# This guy was high-voltage trouble

Ross Chandler was the kind of carelessly arrogant personality that Karen was so drawn to—over and over again. The kind of reckless guy who admired her police work and understood the thrills of risk-taking.

But she'd come to spy. To stand in judgment on her child's adoptive parent.

One hard assessing look into his glittering eyes told her that he was already mentally making love to her.

And he knew she knew.

**Leandra Logan** admits she took this story straight out of today's headlines because she, herself, has never had a secret baby. Nevertheless, she found the idea exciting in its possibilities and consequences. While Leandra is best known for her breezy, comic romps, *Happy Birthday, Baby* was a chance to write dramatic emotions—and Leandra admits it is the first time one of her own stories made her cry!

## Books by Leandra Logan

HARLEQUIN TEMPTATION

# HAPPY BIRTHDAY, BABY

## LEANDRA LOGAN

## *Harlequin Books*

TORONTO • NEW YORK • LONDON
AMSTERDAM • PARIS • SYDNEY • HAMBURG
STOCKHOLM • ATHENS • TOKYO • MILAN
MADRID • WARSAW • BUDAPEST • AUCKLAND

To Birgit Davis-Todd and Malle Vallik

For all you do, this one's for you!

ISBN 0-373-25619-1

HAPPY BIRTHDAY, BABY

Copyright © 1994 by Mary Schultz.

# 1

HEADS TURNED as the young policewoman moved with a sense of urgency through the gleaming corridor of the Las Vegas General Hospital's cancer ward. But the gazes following her progress held sympathic acknowledgment rather than fearful surprise. While the officer in the tan uniform was in stark contrast with her sea of white surroundings, she was not an unexpected visitor or, for that matter, a new one. After her daily visits for four solid weeks, the hospital personnel knew full well that Officer Karen Bradford wasn't here on official business to chase a suspect or corner a witness. The enemy was death, and the days of chasing cures and cornering life were at long last over.

Karen was here to say goodbye to the only person on earth who loved her thoroughly and unconditionally—her aunt Irene.

Milly, the plump, middle-aged nurse who headed the floor, was waiting for Karen outside Irene's closed door. "Thank goodness you got here in time," she greeted in hushed compassion.

Karen's lovely face crumpled with grief under Milly's concerned perusal. On the job and in the presence of her aunt, she suppressed her feelings. It was only with the hospital staff that Karen felt free to unveil the true extent of her turmoil.

"Can you manage?" Milly questioned.

"Yes. I appreciate your persistence in tracking me down."

"When Irene Bradford makes a request, people hop to," Milly whispered. "She's quite a lady."

Karen's brilliant blue eyes shimmered in pride. "She is at that."

"I'll be right outside if you need me," Milly assured her, giving Karen's arm a pat. "But she told me not to interrupt."

With a fortifying sigh, Karen entered the sickroom. The wide door slid shut again, sealing off aunt and niece in a bubble of stuffy silence.

"Aunt Irene? Can you hear me?"

The petite woman tucked snugly beneath the covers blinked at the sound of Karen's voice. There wasn't much left of the once fit and feisty Irene Bradford. Her frame was rail thin, her hair a thin tuft of white, and her face a shallow, wrinkled shell.

Karen slipped into the chair beside the bed and leaned over to take Irene's trembling fingers in hers for a brief squeeze. She set the old woman's limp hand back on the mattress, thinking how firm a hand it had been guiding Karen through her final years of adolescence, how strong and sure it had waved whenever Irene sought to make a point. But Irene's vitality was nothing more than a memory now, drained away with age and illness.

When Irene opened her eyes several minutes later, Karen was hovering over her, smoothing the already-tidy bedding. The old woman managed to curve her lined mouth as she noted Karen's uniform. "You were working...." she murmured with unmistakable respect.

"Yes," Karen admitted, easing back into the chair. "But I've always been game for a little hooky, you know."

"Thought we cured you of that," her aunt countered with a shadow of her old sass.

Karen laughed a little, knowing that Irene would expect it. But her voice was forced and choked. And so loud in the stillness.

"What time is it?" Irene rasped.

"Around ten o'clock," Karen reported with a quick glance at her watch. Even in her final moments, Irene would want to know the hour. She'd always prided herself on being a punctual, orderly person completely focused on time and place.

Irene swallowed hard. "Need to talk."

"Conserve your energy," Karen urged, reaching out to stroke her aunt's fevered brow.

"Called you here to listen, girl," Irene insisted.

"Now, Irene," Karen hastened to protest, "after all the hashing we've done, there just can't be much of anything left to say. Please try to conserve your strength."

Irene's gray eyes gleamed keenly. "What for?"

"Damn you, old woman!" Karen cried softly. "Do you want to die?"

"Yes." Irene licked her lips and coughed slightly. "It's my time."

"You and your obsession with time." Karen knew better than to wimp out now. Irene would hate it. She admired only strength and courage.

"Need to talk now," she persisted in distress.

Salty tears stung Karen's eyes, blurring her vision. She slipped a hankie out of her pocket and dabbed her lashes. "Have I ever dared not to listen?"

Irene shifted her head on the pillow, as though summoning strength. Or was it an attempt to mentally assemble the proper words? Karen couldn't imagine what could be so important. They'd spent hours here together during the past few weeks, after Irene's lung cancer had finally zapped away her independence, driving her into this hospital bed with round-the-clock care.

"Remember when you came to me, girl...."

"Yes, of course," she assured her with a sniff.

A decade had passed since sixteen-year-old Karen had arrived at her spinster aunt's doorstep. Milton Bradford, Karen's father and Irene's brother, had died of cancer himself sometime before. Karen's mother, a tragic agoraphobic, had finally washed her hands of her daughter. Karen could vividly remember standing on the front stoop of Irene's modest green stucco home, with two large suitcases and a truckload of emotional baggage. A homeless rebel. A pregnant teenager one step away from the system and foster care.

The battle of wills had begun then and there with Karen's tests and Irene's consequences. Karen eventually found herself tutored well on the subjects of discipline and routine. In the worst of times as in the best of times, Irene was consistent. This guarantee gave Karen the sense of security that had been lacking in her upbringing.

"I hope I wasn't too bad in the beginning, Auntie," she murmured, biting back a sob behind her hankie.

"Not bad, Karen. A bit wild. Without direction." She struggled to inhale. "Deserved a chance."

"Shall I call the nurse?" Karen asked in a rush of panic.

"No." Her head lolled on the pillow. "Only fuss."

"I want to thank you again, for all you did."

"Don't . . . hate me."

"How could I ever hate you?" Karen lamented with a toss of her blond head, the rebel of old emerging for a brief moment. "You saved my life. Loved me enough to stand up to me."

"Tough love," Irene croaked with a wan look. "Tough on both of us. Hate to leave you alone. Now that you've grown so easy to . . . manipulate."

"Very funny," Karen retorted with a small rueful smile. "But believe me, I'm not alone. I have my friends on the force and I have Judge Stewart."

Irene's withered face strained in yearning. "Stew is your friend. Remember. Please."

Karen had teased her aunt many a time about the Honorable Judge Franklin Stewart, known to his friends as Stew. Confidants since college, neither one had ever married. He'd been kind enough to slip into the role of surrogate father, steering her to a career in law enforcement, the sort of job where she could put her daring and energies to good use.

Karen clucked wistfully. "It's time to stop worrying about me, Irene. You did a tremendous job. I turned out fine!"

Irene swallowed with effort, obviously determined to continue. "When you came. With child."

Karen's heart ached with the memory, buried deep in a tiny secret cache where a vigil light burned eternally for the baby she'd lost during delivery, the baby she'd never even laid eyes upon. It was a subject that had been closed between them for a decade, since the day Karen had found herself in this very hospital, a child bearing a child.

"Such a foolish mistake, Auntie," she said.

"Empty girl, looking for love," Irene rationalized. "We all slip up...."

Karen didn't recall such understanding at the time, only tight-lipped tolerance. But the picture as a whole was all that mattered. Irene came through as a guardian and mentor, opening up her home, sharing her possessions and her wisdom. It had to be inconvenient, considering that she'd lived her entire adult life alone by choice. "You held your head high in spite of my condition," Karen complimented gently. "It had to take courage."

"Coward," Irene blurted out in feeble anguish.

Karen gasped in amazement. "Not you! Not ever!"

Irene nodded insistently. "Tried to teach you love. Give you fresh start."

"You succeeded beyond all hope," Karen hastened to assure her. "Had my baby lived, she, too, would have shared in the best."

Emotion played across the old woman's face. In these last moments of life, through all her pain, she was waging a fierce internal battle. A tightness gripped Karen's throat as she watched her aunt. Watched and waited.

Seconds stretched to minutes. An intense undercurrent seized the silent room, separate from the veil of death hovering overhead. What on earth could the staid Irene Bradford be struggling with in this final stage?

Stressed taut from lack of sleep and endless worry, Karen felt she could shatter into a million pieces. Irene wasn't one to ramble or reminisce. She was leading up to something, trying to tell her something.

"What's on your mind, Irene?" she prodded softly, desperately. Maybe Irene was attempting to say the simple words, "I love you, Karen." Irene had never actually said them, not in all the years they'd shared a home. She'd expressed them in a million different ways, but never officially voiced them. That would certainly take courage. And it would be a gift Karen would never forget. "I love you, Auntie," she whispered.

Irene's eyes flew open. "See Stew. Love you. . . ."

With a quiet sigh, Irene Bradford was gone.

Characteristically, Irene had managed to have the last word, even this final time. But had there been more to the message?

IRENE'S COMFORTABLE SMALL home was in the residential section of Las Vegas, miles away from the glittering energy of the strip. It looked very much like all the other stucco ramblers on the flat tract of desert. But inside, it was uniquely personalized, vividly reflecting the old woman who had bought it new nearly forty years ago.

Karen wandered the rooms later that evening, reliving memories in a fog of grief. This had been her home, her shelter from the storm for such a long time. She had moved out for a short while after graduating from the police academy and taken an apartment with a friend. But she had ended up returning when Irene's health had begun its final decline. They had reversed roles, with her now playing the caregiver.

There were so many things to put in order, she thought ruefully, staring down at the untouched meal the next-door neighbor had set out for her on the kitchen table. Closing the book on a loved one's personal and business affairs was a sad and tedious task.

Knowing she couldn't swallow a bite, Karen turned on her heel and headed for the small spare bedroom that had served as Irene's office. She sat down in the creaky spring-loaded chair, placing her palms on Irene's old oak desk.

Irene was already retired when Karen moved in, having enjoyed an illustrious career as a high school English teacher in this very neighborhood. Her only request of the school was that they reward her with the sturdy wooden desk and chair from her classroom. Irene had often retold the tale, claiming the students had been so intent on getting rid of her that the football team had lifted her and the furniture out the door on her last day of teaching.

In reality most of the kids respected Miss Bradford's no-nonsense policy. The house was littered with small mementos of her students. They had families of their own now, but they still remembered old Miss Bradford at the holidays. Many stopped by to see her, and insisted she sit behind her desk, just for a moment of nostalgia.

They would all come this one last time—to the funeral service, to the house. They would retell their own stories of how Miss Bradford had boosted them onto the honor roll by making a B + an A −, or how she'd made herself available evenings for a little private tutoring—sometimes even without the knowledge of parents and school officials. Or how she'd prodded and bullied them into peak performance in the classroom.

They would come to say goodbye. They would wonder what she'd said at the end. Surely something dignified. Something worthy of an English scholar who was never at a loss for words.

Karen leaned over the desk and buried her head in her arms. Immersed in the taste of her own salty tears and the scent of lemon furniture polish, she allowed the sorrow to consume her.

What would she tell those anxious former students? Aunt Irene had struggled with her words in those final moments. She'd stumbled, stuttered and gasped. Karen would have to find a way to explain in some vague way that wouldn't disappoint too much. Irene had been a shell of her former self, a far cry from the vibrant educator they remembered.

Karen sat motionless for a long time, replaying the scene at Irene's bedside in her mind. Amazingly, it was a helpful process. Irene had said goodbye, had spoken of love.

But she'd also spoken of hate, of cowardice. Karen wondered if there had been more. If Irene had intended to reveal something important.

Judge Franklin Stewart was the key. Irene had steered her in that direction. Unfortunately, he'd missed Irene's final hours, having been out of town for the past two days tending to some business. Though the seventy-three-year-old had stepped down from the bench nearly a decade ago, he still kept busy with a part-time law practice. His secretary, Justine Wilson, had contacted him with the sorrowful news. He'd promised to return tonight.

Anxious for a comforting word, she picked up the telephone at her elbow and punched in Stew's home number. The sound of his smooth, dignified voice brought her immeasurable comfort.

"Ah, Karen, I just arrived home. Thought perhaps it was too late to call."

"I was thinking of going to bed," she confessed. "But I just wanted to make sure you were back safe and sound."

"Yes, of course. Please accept my most sincere sympathies, my dear."

"Please accept mine," she returned softly. "I know how much she meant to you."

"Yes, yes," he agreed wistfully. "We've been a family for quite some time now, the three of us. We shall miss her together."

There was a brief pause on the line as they struggled with their own separate emotions.

"Everything is arranged," Karen reported. "The service is tomorrow at her church. I'm having the luncheon here at the house afterward."

Stew chuckled wryly. "The little organizer planned it all herself, didn't she?"

Karen sniffed, drawing a smile. "She always did like to run the show."

"The end must have been difficult for you," he ventured quietly.

"Irene helped me through it," Karen assured him. With a hasty breath, she forged ahead with her inquiry. "Stew, you have all of her papers in order, don't you?"

"Of course, dear! Justine said she sent them over earlier in the day."

Karen eyed the bulging accordion envelope on the desk beside Irene's pencil jar. "Yes, I have them right here."

"We can take a few moments tomorrow to sort through them. There isn't much to deal with really, aside from her house, her savings and a small life insurance policy. And you know about her endowment to the high school."

"Is that all, Stew?"

"Yes," he assured her with a measure of bewilderment. "Do you have cause to think differently?"

"I know this probably sounds sentimentally silly, but I feel that Irene was trying to tell me something just before the end."

"Really? How odd."

Karen frowned, blinking away the moistness blurring her vision. There was a definite catch in his voice. Was he concealing something, or was he just feeling the fallout from what had to be one of the most tragic losses of his life?

"She mentioned a slipup, Stew."

"Our Irene? Such nonsense, Karen! Surely you are mistaken."

"No, she weighed every word quite carefully. I truly believe that she was working up to some sort of revelation. That if she'd had a few moments more, she would've gotten to the point."

"Even in this betting town, you'd have gotten few takers on that one," Stew retorted. "Irene Bradford laid her cards out on the table the instant they were dealt to her. She never withheld an opinion, never offered apologies."

"I think she cherished our approval, our admiration," Karen asserted in a rush of fervency. "It took me years to gain that insight, but I'm sure that beneath her dictatorial demeanor she cared what we thought of her. And at the end, in keeping with her systematic ways, she wanted to exit with everything properly filed away."

"You understood Irene quite well, my dear. But you are wrong about this."

Karen bit her lip. There was a distinct thread of annoyance in his tone. "She was fretting over something.

Seemed concerned that I might come to hate her. It seems like a mystery worth exploring—"

"Delirium in no uncertain terms!" he proclaimed with courtroom vigor. "You are only making her parting harder on yourself," he continued on a quieter note. "It is always difficult to accept the death of one so strong and vibrant. It's natural for you to ask the question, 'Is that all there is?' But there is nothing more to Irene."

"But she seemed so—"

"I advise you to accept the realities of the situation," he interrupted with a trace of briskness. "Irene based her whole life on dealing with the tangible. She would be most proud if you took her example to heart now in this vulnerable time and resisted indulging in imaginative flights."

Karen hung up the telephone a short time later, hoping with all her heart that it was her overactive imagination. But Irene had been quite lucid before her death. And Karen was sure she had been trying to deliver an important message, carefully rationing her words as she ran out of strength.

Irene had really started to choke up when they'd begun to talk about Karen's arrival and her pregnancy. Could it be that Irene had been secretly mortified by her niece's condition, that she had been nursing guilt over her feelings all this time? Irene had certainly always prided herself on being as nonjudgmental as possible concerning all the youngsters in her domain.

Swallowing a yawn, Karen reached out for the thick envelope containing Irene's legacy and pulled it to the center of the desk. A final assignment that needed a final grade.

# 2

BY TWO O'CLOCK the following afternoon, Irene Bradford was laid to rest. Scores of friends and former students, as well as some of Karen's police force cronies
had gathered in her home for fond reminiscences. Irene,
in characteristic form, had left explicit instructions
about this last hurrah. Karen was to wear her black
sheath dress with the neckline scooped low enough to
display Irene's cherished opal pendant. A gift from Stew
dating back to their college days, the silver piece was
only modestly valuable, but the family's only real
heirloom.

And then there was the meal. Irene had specified
what should be served and how it should be served.
Everyone mingling in the kitchen and living and dining rooms was, as per instructions, using a mug from
Irene's extensive collection. Each ceramic cup held
special significance. Each one was a gift from a student. They came in numerous colors and shapes and
were imprinted with a variety of messages. Most of
them had a scholarly compliment, such as Best Teacher
or Excellent Educator, and were shaped like apples or
bookends. But some had logos from the casinos along
the Las Vegas strip and were molded in provocative
shapes of showgirl torsos and bottoms.

Irene added each one to her collection with pride,
aware that many of the parents of her charges worked
on the strip. She enjoyed bridging the gap between their

professions with a cup of coffee. She never gambled on anything more than her students' will to learn, but she acknowledged their diverse backgrounds as part of life.

Karen went through the crowd one last time with a carafe of Irene's favorite hazelnut-flavored roast, discovering that everyone had had their fill. It was a hot, arid spring afternoon, and the antiquated air-conditioning system didn't even come close to coping with the rising body heat. But all those present had partaken of the steamy brew, knowing that it was Irene's wish.

Things soon began to break up. People came to say goodbye with handclasps and kisses. Karen noted that Stew had stationed himself near the front door to take care of the departing guests. She paused to study the tall, dapper, grief-stricken judge with a mixture of sympathy and suspicion. She had been so troubled by their conversation and by his defensive attitude that she'd spent half the night pouring over everything in the bulging brown envelope. There had been nothing unusual among Irene's papers. But what had she really expected to find? If Stew was concealing something, he wouldn't have presented her with black-and-white proof!

Karen returned to the kitchen and slipped the coffeepot back on the burner. She heard a slight rap on the back door and turned to find Stew's secretary, Justine Wilson, easing inside with a large manila envelope under her arm.

"Hate to intrude on your gatherin'," she said in hushed apology, pushing the door with her shapely hip.

Karen smiled fondly at the statuesque woman dressed in the yellow cotton dress. A former showgirl with ebony skin and exotic almond eyes, Justine was a striking adornment at the front desk of Judge Stewart's small law office. She was also the ultimate gal Friday, with her finger in every brief, her ear to every phone call—and the ideal person to take investigative action concerning Irene's affairs.

"You are not intruding, Justine. I called you." Karen eyed the secretary's envelope with anticipation.

"Wisely, so it seems," Justine said with a small nod. "You were absolutely right about those misplaced papers being filed in his confidential cabinet. Of course, I had to read them to verify that they were the ones," she added on a contrite note. "So I know . . ."

"Of course," Karen demurred, tucking her shimmery golden hair behind her ear to avoid direct eye contact. Karen had to follow through, pretend that she knew what Justine had just discovered. Her suggestion that the confidential file had even existed had been a shot in the dark. She had called Justine shortly before the service, when she'd been certain that the judge wouldn't be on hand to intervene in the search.

She was a heartbeat away from the truth.

Karen turned to the police officers lingering near the old chrome table. Along with their superior, Chief George Bradley, they were waiting to say goodbye. Karen accepted their hugs and condolences, then turned back to Justine. They were now alone in the kitchen.

"I don't know how the judge overlooked something so important," Justine said on a note of tenderness. "Especially considerin' how much it meant to Irene at the end and all."

"Yes, as I told you, she was so insistent that I have all the records."

"She was quite the organizer," Justine agreed. "Guess the judge was just too shook up to think straight."

"Thank goodness we have you," Karen said, gratefully accepting the envelope.

"Well, I'd better get back." Justine glanced at the gold watch on her wrist. "I imagine the judge won't be returning to the office anytime soon. Not if you're going to discuss those documents."

Karen's hands shook as she unclasped the envelope. She hadn't enjoyed bluffing her way into this information, but knowing of Justine's unwavering loyalty to Stew, she'd been given no alternative. Neither one of them would appreciate her trickery, but she was desperate. Somehow she had the feeling that a cruel trick had been played on her a long time ago. She was aware that Justine had paused at the threshold to look at her.

Karen saw the certificate that confirmed her wildest guess.

Justine's dramatic slashed brows arched in concern. "You all right, Karen? This is what you wanted, isn't it?"

"Oh, yes," she replied breathlessly, her heart hammering in her chest. "Thank you very much, Justine."

Karen returned to the living room in a sleepwalker's stride, the envelope pressed against the bodice of her simple black dress. There were only a few lingering guests, friends of Stew's. They were hovering near the front door on the verge of departing. Karen thanked them for coming and glided toward Irene's small office. With a fortifying breath, she closed the door after her, then raced for the desk, tearing off the flap of the envelope as she went.

She sank down into the smooth wooden chair, spilling papers over the polished desktop. Her pounding temples threatened to burst as she shifted through the remnants of her own heritage.

*She was a mother! Of a real-life baby girl.*

Hot tears sprang to her eyes, stinging her lids, blurring her vision. The baby she believed dead for ten long years had lived, walked on the planet unbeknownst to her all this time!

Relief and fury surged through her, causing her breath to come in rapid, forceful heaves.

Baby Bradford. Six pounds, nine ounces. Blue eyes. Blond hair.

Father unknown.

With clenched fists, she stared down at the statistics typed neatly into the boxes on the form. Time became relative as she slowly slipped back into the past, reliving her brief stint as a mother-to-be. The pregnancy, the labor, the news of the stillborn child. And then there were the subsequent birthdays to endure. May fifteenth. So near Mother's Day each and every year. The double whammy. The memories of her own dysfunctional mother and the death of the daughter she'd never even seen always managed to engulf her in a sea of despair.

There had been no one to lean on. Irene had never been very good with overwhelming emotion of any kind. She'd refused to dig that deep inside herself, and therefore found the passionate responses of others overdone. Irene would stand near, but clear, during those turbulent spells, like a tall sturdy oak in a rainstorm. A person could expect to find some shelter beneath her branches, but there was little warmth or protection from the elements. The storm would eventually pass and the status quo of the household returned.

Irene had kept the secret year after year throughout it all. Now it appeared that those painful anniversaries of death had been joyous celebrations of life for her own little girl! It left her numb with bittersweet relief.

The next time Karen looked up, Stew was standing near the window overlooking the front yard. The afternoon sun was slanting through the window, highlighting the lines at his mouth and eyes, his thinning hair. Despite his age, he still cut a strong figure in his black suit and wing tips.

"You lied to me, Stew."

He turned, his expression grave. With a trace of defeat, his gaze fell to the familiar envelope lying on the desk. "I followed Irene's direction on the matter."

"She wanted me to know! Tried to tell me before she slipped away. But even last night, after she was gone, you stuck to the lie about my baby!" She tried to bite back the sob in her throat, but it erupted in a squeak just the same.

"I—don't believe it's what she really wanted," he maintained, keeping his chin high as he moved closer. "It wasn't like her to renege on a decision."

"Oh, you two always thought you had the answers to every damn blasted thing!" she cried out, jumping to her feet. "But you were tampering with my life! My child's life!" Resting knuckles on the desktop, she leaned over to pin him with her large eyes of liquid blue fire. "What do you have to say about that, Judge? How would you handle such a case in your courts?"

There was no vicious edge to the challenge. Rather, her voice was small, husky, full of desperation and disappointment. The judge was instantly reminded of the sassy, vulnerable girl who'd stormed into Irene's life a whole decade ago. She'd dared them to love her. They'd taken that dare and won. They'd all won. If only he could make her see that.

"You must try to understand, Karen." His voice was mild, but full of steady strength. "You were a teenage rebel when Irene took you in. A pregnant, misguided child. Irene did her best."

Karen lifted her chin with a sniff. "I appreciate Irene's dedication to duty, but there is more to mothering than that! Despite her teaching background, her rapport with her students, she didn't understand about a mother's bond. Didn't understand why I would've liked to have had a say about my baby."

"Has it occurred to you that perhaps she was frightened?"

Her fragile jawline sagged. "Frightened of my baby?"

Stew shook his regal head with a wry smile. "Frightened of you, Karen."

"No way."

"Oh, yes, she was," Stew insisted with a knowing nod. "In the beginning anyway. Unfortunately, you two were thrown together at a most crucial crossroad of your life. It was all so foreign to her, you see. You were a youngster about to be a mother and Irene wasn't the maternal type. She was determined to relate to you, Karen. But it had to be as a challenging student, not as a daughter."

Karen sank back into the chair, as though the wind had been knocked out of her. "She approached me as a student in need?" she whispered bleakly.

"Isn't so bad, really," Stew said comfortingly. "This house was bursting with grateful students today. She gave in her own way, dear. Admittedly it wasn't with gushy warmth—"

"She didn't understand sentiment," Karen blurted out sadly.

"There you are wrong, young lady," Stew scolded with a pointed finger. "Irene felt these things, but could not bring herself to express them. She was a remarkable woman. Insightful enough to realize that she would be an inept mother. Realized that not every female had strong maternal instincts long before there were a million books written on the subject. She wanted to teach, to give of herself, but she didn't want to settle down and have a family."

"So she really didn't want me."

"Stop talking nonsense! I'm not telling you these things to make you feel that you were a burden to her. Rather, I'd like you to view this whole situation from her position. She cared for you, Karen. But she was already sixty-five when your baby was born. Just imagine. She had retired from teaching, intent on pursuing modest hobbies on a modest pension. Suddenly her whole agenda was turned upside down. The best she could do was take you in and put you on the structured program she'd used in the classroom."

"And my baby..."

Stew inhaled sharply, as though weighing his words. "She gave you both a fresh start."

Resentment and grief warred within Karen as she examined her situation. She'd lost the only woman who had ever given a whit about her. But that woman had lied to her, given away her child.

"I have a right to the facts," she announced before once again turning her attention to the documents on the desk.

Judge Stewart placed a palm over the splay of papers. "Please, allow me to tell you. It is all there, but

Irene would want you to learn of everything with a slant of subjectivity. You owe me that, after sneaking around to get the file."

Karen sat back, placing her hands in her lap. "All right, Stew."

After years of performing in the courtroom, the judge had a habit of pacing when compelled to speak on an issue. True to form, he began to walk the length of the desk as though it were a jury box. Which, in a way, it was.

In her line of work Karen was accustomed to interviewing reluctant citizens and frequently asked leading questions. "So, the baby was born alive and well," she prodded.

"Oh, yes. Lovely, fair-haired like yourself."

Karen bit her full lower lip, struggling to keep her composure. She dreaded the realities about to be presented, but she also longed to hear the truth.

"The baby was placed with an affluent couple here in Nevada."

"Did Irene go through the Christian charities?"

"She intended to," Stew began slowly, "but an opportunity suddenly arose from a private party. Through the prestigious firm of Willis and Darnell."

"Willis is your cousin, isn't he?" Karen mused.

"Yes," he admitted. "In confidence, Carl Willis told me he had a client who had miscarried and desperately wanted to adopt. He'd known the woman's family for years. Boston bluebloods, I understand. Anyway, she had married into a family of local entrepreneurs—"

"Gamblers?" Karen frantically questioned.

"Resort owners."

"Local?"

"Lake Tahoe. The name's there, on some of the paperwork. Chandler. Ross and Margo Chandler. Ross and his brother own the Pleasure Palace Resort up there."

"She sold my baby to these Chandlers, didn't she?"

"Now, Karen—"

"Tell me the truth, Stew!"

"I'm trying to." Stew leaned over to sift through the documents on the desk. "They paid your hospital bill. It's all here—" He inhaled sharply as she snatched a paper from his hand.

Her sapphire eyes widened in horror as she read it. "My signature is on here with Irene's!"

"Yes."

"Why— I didn't know what I was doing! I was doped up afterward!"

"You were a very frail young lady," he hastened to clarify. "Everything moved swiftly."

So what the hell was the huge rush? Karen wondered. She wasn't going anywhere, nor was the baby. "This hospital bill wasn't all that large," she muttered, pushing several of the papers around on the desktop for closer scrutiny.

"It's the way adoptions work," he explained, noticeably uncomfortable under her piercing inspection. "It's the legal way."

Something clicked inside her head. Stew's unease and the small amount of money involved just didn't seem to add up to a smooth aboveboard transaction. Stew was such an upright, moralistic jurist. But he was just a man where it concerned Irene.

She fingered the pendant that he'd given Irene so long ago, thinking how he'd been forever the besotted schoolboy under his love's beaming gaze. If he had ever slipped out of line, it would've been for Irene and nobody else. And this was the time to catch him at it, when he was weary and vulnerable.

"The Chandlers paid a lot, didn't they?" she asked. Her deliberate abruptness caught him off guard, and his aristocratic features crumbled.

"Yes, Karen," he confessed heavily. "That was how it was. They wanted your baby and paid top dollar for her. A secret cash payment to insure Irene's cooperation and discretion. Mrs. Chandler was here the very night you gave birth. She and the baby were gone by morning."

Karen's lower lip trembled. "Just up and left with my child."

"Haven't you ever wondered, m'dear, where the money for your support came from?"

Karen's hands fluttered helplessly. "Irene never spoke of finances, Stew. I had no reason to question the resources that kept us going. I certainly had no cause to suspect that it was from the sale of my baby."

"Irene gained nothing by the sale," Stew swiftly clarified. "It all was funneled into your future! Every cent was yours. Irene never... never would've had the funds to see you through."

"I worked, even as a teenager."

"My dear girl, that wouldn't begin to cover your expenses. And you didn't work in the beginning. You were traumatized after the birth, remember? And you had your studies to attend to." When her fierce glare didn't waver, he added, "I gladly chipped in to the cause on occasion. You've always been like a daughter to me."

"Don't try to get me gooey about our relationship," she snapped back.

"We've always been gooey about it," he insisted. "Had Irene agreed to marry me and give me children, I would've been the happiest chap on earth. But since she didn't, I was thrilled to have you. You were my two girls, my family."

Karen bristled under his affectionate look. "I am so damn mad at you right now!"

"But you love me as I love you," he said quietly. "We wanted to do what was right, believe me. Agonized over it. We even searched for that louse who fathered the child."

"You looked for Larry?" Karen frowned, remembering the shallow ladies' man fifteen years her senior who had taken her virginity. She had been drifting in and out of her mother's house at that time, skipping school, singing with a lounge act on the strip. Larry had been a suave tourist on a gambling spree who had spotted her on stage. He'd easily tapped into her vulnerabilities, her yearning for love and acceptance. For the next two weeks, he had seduced her body and spirit with passionate lovemaking, honeyed promises and lavish nightclubbing. And then he was gone. Just packed up one day and disappeared. Shortly thereafter, Karen's lovesickness had turned to morning sickness. Her own mother had broken down completely and Irene had gallantly stepped in.

"I'm sure Larry wasn't even his real name," Stew commented on a hardened note. "Not much to go on in any case."

"Well, I'm glad you didn't locate him," Karen declared flatly. "The older, wiser woman in me now realizes he wasn't worth a second look. And he probably already had a family of his own someplace."

"Yes," Stew sagely agreed. "A family who probably figured he was a salesman on the road, rather than a professional gambler." His features softened as he sought her understanding. "I only bring it up, Karen, because I want you to understand that Irene and I were not behaving like heartless monsters. We viewed your pregnancy as a crisis and acted on your behalf in the best way we knew how."

Karen sighed softly, rubbing her moist eyes. "Those days seem like another life in a lot of ways."

"Just my point, dear," Stew pressed earnestly. He rounded the desk to angle his arm around her shoulders. "This is your life. Our life." He placed a light kiss on her suntanned temple. "A real daughter couldn't mean more to me than you do. If I close my eyes, I can imagine what you must have been like even as a toddler."

"Oh, Stew!" she scoffed gently.

After a pause, he continued on a more serious note. "I know Irene wasn't demonstrative, but don't allow yourself to wallow in what might have been. I think you've been quite satisfied with the time spent under our care. Don't allow these revelations about the baby and Irene's teacher-pupil approach to parenting to spoil the good things."

"I need time to think, to absorb it all," she admitted, tipping her head against his snowy white shirt.

He stroked the length of her long golden hair. "Life is a journey and we all have our destinies. It's unwise to fiddle with fate."

Karen raised her head, regarding him with a doleful look. "That corny expression tells me that you're scared witless about what I'm going to do next."

"Irene and I have been in a witless state concerning your behavior for the past ten years," he replied evasively.

She clucked in chiding as she smoothed his gray cashmere lapel. "You stalled me with all you had on this stuff."

The judge held his regal chin high. "I plead the Fifth Amendment."

"I want to know if my baby's happy," she declared stubbornly.

Stew cupped the curve of her cheek in his hand for a brief moment. "Tampering with other people's lives can be risky, Karen."

"But she's mine!" she flared with renewed emotion.

"The only thing worse than a thankless child is a selfish parent," he cautioned, his pale eyes full of reprimand. "This is a delicate matter for all concerned. The happiness of many is at issue here."

"I realize that!"

"You are a hands-on woman," he continued. "You seize the moment, the day, the cause. It makes you a sharp, effective cop and a vibrant, compassionate woman—"

"But I am a lethal weapon when I want something?" she cut in with annoyance.

He nodded slowly, looking every bit his age at that moment. "You cannot go and seize that girl, take her in your arms and give her a decade's worth of love." He paused, then added, "Well, you could manage it, but you mustn't."

Karen had a great respect for Stew's opinions. So great a respect that she found herself in the rare state of indecision.

"Just a formality," Justine trilled proudly. "You're really in already."

"I was thinking more along the lines of cocktail waitress!"

"You may as well use your voice," Justine declared with flat practicality. "And this opening is perfect for you. Their regular singer in the Starlite Lounge is ill with some sudden throat ailment, so they're looking for a week-long fill-in starting this Friday. I explained that you're a friend who's worked some of the smaller lounges here. A friend who needs some time away from the Vegas scene. That's the truth, anyway."

"But a lounge act . . ."

"There were plenty of other job openings, of course," Justine assured her dolefully. "You know people constantly move in and out of those places. But I can guarantee that you won't get near your girl if you're serving drinks or washing windows. You need to be out front. In a slinky dress. Grabbing the spotlight."

Karen's golden brows arched in amazement. "What?"

"The quickest way to that girl is through her father," Justine said bluntly.

"Play up to a married man?"

Justine inhaled in hesitation. "Well, he isn't exactly married anymore. . . ."

"My daughter's adoptive parents are divorced?"

"Have been for four years. The child, Wendy, lives with Ross at the resort."

"Wendy doesn't live with the mother at all?" Karen queried bleakly.

Justine shrugged, her brown eyes warm with sympathy. "Apparently Ross fought for custody and won. I called the judge's cousin, Carl Willis, the one who

"It wouldn't be that difficult to get an update on the family without ever going near them," Stew said.

Karen flashed him a vague, Mona Lisa smile. Such a proposal didn't even begin to cover her needs. It disappointed her that he thought she should settle for such an inadequate crumb. But she needed time and space to come up with a plausible plan that would best serve her and her daughter. "I think we should just let this go for today," she murmured evenly. "We both need some rest."

His sigh was heavy with an odd mixture of reluctance and relief. "All right. Just accept that it's natural for you to feel overwrought. You've been keeping vigil at Irene's hospital bed for a long time, and now that you've had to absorb this unexpected news . . ."

"I will think before I act," she promised, then bit her lip to quell the excitement pulsing through her.

She actually had a daughter!

A daughter who was having a tenth birthday.

She would see that girl. Somehow, someday, she would.

"THE JUDGE WILL KILL ME dead when he finds out that I helped you, Karen."

"You have more lives than a cat where your boss is concerned, Justine. Guess we both do." Karen grinned up at Judge Stewart's secretary from the Wilsons' wooden swing, accepting a mug of steaming coffee from the older woman. Karen had just come off the night shift the following Wednesday and was relaxing on the front porch of Justine's elegant town house. She was still dressed in her uniform and her squad car was parked out front.

Forty-eight hours had passed since Karen had promised Stew she'd proceed with caution concerning her baby. It seemed like forty-eight years since she'd told that lie. She would see that child. Touch her if at all possible...

"You couldn't help but come to the aid of another mother," Karen consoled her confidently, balancing the mug on the slender bow of her thigh. "Having two boys of your own, you understand my pain, probably more clearly than I understand it myself."

Justine nodded as she buttoned her white blazer. "Yes! And now I have to go and face the man in his office. Pretend his reprimand for rifling through his personal files has made me a wiser and more humble assistant."

Karen wrinkled her nose in discontent. "After his subterfuge with Irene, I think I'm entitled to a few secrets of my own." Under Justine's concerned look, she added, "I only involved you out of necessity. This matter was too delicate to take through regular channels at the station. Somebody would've gotten curious and the confidentiality of the matter would've been jeopardized."

"Well, I'm happy to hear you using words like delicate," Justine said with a humph, backing away from her front door as her sons, aged seven and eight, barreled out of the house with their knapsacks and lunch boxes.

"Hey, Karen!" they chorused. "Can we have a ride to school in the squad car? Daddy says it's okay with him."

"Not today," Justine broke in before Karen could reply in the affirmative. Kissing them each on the forehead, she steered them down the porch stairs. "Get to the bus stop pronto." With whoops and scampered down the sidewalk.

Justine shook her head with a sigh, the long, lean figure onto the swing beside Ka as much as I dislike the idea of sidestep Stewart, working outside the channels, I agre have no choice. You don't need statistics on dlers. You need gossip. You need an in."

Karen had already discussed a course of ac Justine. In order to get an intimate look at he ter's circumstances, Karen planned to take a s cation and seek out temporary employment Chandlers' Lake Tahoe resort. It wouldn't be d to step in undetected. She intended to drop the from Bradford and alter her résumé to fit whatev was open. Justine, being an exshowgirl, had connections in Tahoe and, fortunately, a good o the Pleasure Palace.

"So did you speak to your friend?" Karen as hopefully, sipping her coffee. "Did you track dov job for me?"

Justine nodded. "Dinah Delray's her name danced together at several of the casinos here i Vegas—before we hit our mid-thirties and were p aside for the fresh young things. Dinah moved Tahoe after that. She's worked her way up throu ranks to entertainment coordinator at the P Palace." Justine's warm brown eyes gleamed wit "It's a big sprawling complex, you know. Sev taurants and lounges. Lots of entertainer spo She said that she'd be more than happy to giv Karen Ford, an audition and free lodging i ployee wing of the hotel."

"An audition?" Karen repeated in a gasp.

handles Margo's affairs, and did a little fishing. Didn't find out much about Margo, aside from the fact that she's difficult and lacking a maternal shine."

"And Ross?"

"He's accustomed to getting what he wants. Guess he wanted that little girl real bad."

Karen's features crumbled with the news. "I had hoped with all of the privileges of wealth and their initial yearning to adopt that the Chandlers' marriage would be a strong one."

Justine raised her slender dark hands in a helpless gesture. "It's an imperfect world, honey."

"But just how imperfect is Wendy's world, I wonder...."

"Best way to find out is by singin' your ole heart out for Daddy Ross," Justine wheedled.

"But I'm so rusty!" Karen objected. "Sure, I did have a stint on stage. At sixteen, during my most misguided months." She pressed her fingers to her temples, steeling herself against the unhappy memories.

"Aside from those painful personal lessons, you learned a lot about stage technique, too, I imagine," Justine asserted, drawing a reluctant nod from Karen. "And you still sing all the time at parties. And there are a dozen good voice teachers in town who would gladly give you a crash refresher course."

"Today?" Karen challenged doubtfully.

Justine's white teeth gleamed behind her bright red lips. "I took the liberty of calling Garnet St. James myself. She's free after two. I told her you'd confirm this morning."

"And the gowns I'll need..."

"You can buy secondhand ones. We both know plenty of girls your size."

Karen ran a hand through her loose hair. "I just don't know if I can pull off a stunt like this...."

"I can't call Dinah Delray back and say you'd rather wash the damn dishes!" Justine sputtered indignantly. "She's going out on a limb for you just because show people help out show people! So I say, on with the show!"

Karen set her empty mug down with a thump on a square slatted table. "You're right, of course! I deserve this break and I'm going to take it."

"Now you're talkin' sense," Justine rejoiced, giving Karen's knee a pat.

"I just can't help wondering...." Karen pondered, slowly rising from the swing. "Why on earth did Margo Chandler want my baby in the first place?"

Justine looked up at Karen's uniformed figure and shrugged. "I don't know. But you'll find out."

A grim, determined smile defined Karen's sultry mouth. "Oh, yes indeed. That's one bet you can take without a qualm."

"So what about the judge?" Justine swiftly asked as Karen started down the porch stairs.

"I'll explain it all in a letter," Karen decided after a thoughtful pause. "I'll drop it by the office tomorrow, on the way to the bus station. It'll be too late for him to stop me then. He can just stew in his own juices for a while."

"Hey, that's cute. Stew can stew." Justine's grin diminished. "He's going to be livid with the both of us. He thinks you should leave this whole thing alone."

"I love Stew with all my heart," Karen said with real feeling. "But he and Irene crossed some hazy moral lines when they sold that baby—not to mention some lawful ones. They tricked me into signing the release form and they took money under the table."

Justine sighed heavily. "I figured as much. Not that he made any such admissions during his lecture on office confidentiality and integrity. But in any case, the cause of motherhood cancels out any lesser loyalties in my mind."

Karen stepped back to give her a hug. "Thanks for everything. I'll make this tussle with Stew up to you somehow."

"Begin by calling us, Karen. I can't face the judge without your promise to call."

"Yes," she relented. "Of course."

"Without delay," Justine pressed. With a grin, she added, "I need to know if Dinah's kept a better figure!"

# 3

KAREN FORD WAS AN AMATEUR.

Ross Chandler watched his new songbird from the back of the Starlite Lounge Friday night with a measure of annoyance. She had a case of stage fright and her voice reflected it. Though no singer himself, his years in the casino business had taught him a lot. For one thing, her breath support was off. She was singing too deeply, hitting the challenging notes with a quavering quality. And she was putting too much emphasis on drawn-out phrases, carrying them through with a noticeable vibration.

Still, she did have charisma. That indefinable something that made the most ambitious entertainers stars.

Leaning against an ivory-colored column, he looked out into the dimness at the audience seated at the clusters of round, linen-covered tables. The crowd was hushed, aside from the clink of glassware and the occasional spurt of conversation. Amazingly, they listened as if mesmerized in a magical bubble drifting from reality.

An impossible feat for a rookie.

An improbable feat for almost anyone.

A grudging respect and admiration smoothed his irritation. Practice and discipline would overcome Karen's weaknesses.

But his main lounge was no place to do it. And Dinah knew that!

Irritation flared anew and he seesawed between disapproval and benediction. This had to be a favor. One of those clannish situations among the show people scattered throughout Nevada. How many times had Dinah pulled this on him during her stint as entertainment coordinator? Well, she'd finally overstepped her limits this time. It was excusable in the smaller lounges here and in their twin resort in Cannes. But the Starlite stage was exclusively reserved for local headliners, like the ailing Tiffany Bond.

He was tempted to put Karen Ford back on the bus she rode in on. If only she weren't scamming the audience into complete captivation, receiving the sort of welcome given his most seasoned singers. He understood, of course. The majority of his guests knew nothing of vibrato and breath support and clannish show folk.

Quite simply, they were moved by Karen Ford and they didn't care why.

Despite her shortcomings, she was shrewd enough to sing from the heart, to break hearts with powerful material. Her voice was a velvet embrace, an intimate infusion of emotion, warming the women, heating the men.

And it was all wrapped up in a glittering blue-and-blond package that dazzled the eye.

Her physical presence enhanced her powers of seductive persuasion with remarkable efficacy. Her glossy hair was a rich tide, curving like a golden wave over her collarbone. Her features were in beautiful balance, like the numerous other women he confronted day after day at his resort. Classically honed cheekbones, full Cupid's-bow lips. Yet she was somehow set apart from all the others by an intriguing individuality. There was a healthy roundness to her cheeks, an appealing fullness. And her lips lacked the sultry puffiness that seemed to be the rage now. Her mouth was generous, without suffering from that all-too-common sulky droop.

She had the face of an angel.

And the body of a vamp.

The royal blue sequined dress was a wise, calculated selection. The slit up the side climbed high, revealing the length of sleek thigh with every step, every shimmy. Impossibly thin twin straps held the form-fitting bodice in place over her breasts. Lush, suntanned breasts, which rose and fell with every breath.

The image was magical.

Ross's lean, muscular body shuddered beneath his elegant evening attire. He could pinpoint each and every contrived nuance in her act. Still, it affected him in the most basic, sensual way, like a cleverly engineered carnival trick.

He wanted to break eye contact, but he was hypnotized by the play of lights, the way the strategically placed beams danced over her. She positively gleamed under them in provocative splendor. His gaze caressed her lustrous hair, the slope of her bare shoulders, then fell to her glittering sequined bottom, so tight, so compact under the tautly pulled fabric.

Ross suddenly had the urge to strip away that fabric to reveal the truth beneath the glitter.

Talk about casino carnival magic!

Talk about basic urges that had no place in this professional arena.

Ross knew he was slipping along thin ice with his lusty musings, but he couldn't help himself. It had been a long time since he'd had such an immediate reaction to a woman. The fact that she was a woman out of place in his place only heightened both his ire and his desire.

He would speak to Dinah about headlining Miss Karen Ford without his consent. And he would speak to Miss Ford herself. Just because . . .

Karen gripped the microphone with a breath of relief. The man in the white dinner jacket and black slacks was finally exiting the lounge.

Ross Chandler. Dinah's brief, concise description had made him easily identifiable. "Dashing Timothy Dalton looks with a cool Clint Eastwood attitude." The entertainment manager had said the big boss would most likely be popping in to check her out. As if Chandler could ever be described as "popping" anywhere at any time! He prowled with an unconscious elegance, moving like a large cat beneath his evening clothes.

A most dangerous-looking daddy.

So just how was he treating her little girl?

Karen was required to sing for another thirty minutes. It was with a feeling of relief and exhaustion that she finally left the stage, weaving her way back to Tiffany Bond's dressing room. She whirled inside, closing the door with the weight of her body. She sagged against the white wood paneling, drawing a long breath.

"Good evening, Miss Ford."

Karen's eyes snapped open. Ross Chandler was seated on the satin-covered love seat beside the dressing table.

"Good evening, Mr. Chandler."

She moved into the room, sizing him up. Ross Chandler was indeed a showman in his own right. He'd boldly taken a front row seat in these private feminine quarters with the deliberate intent of catching her at a spontaneous moment. A private moment when an entertainer preferred some downtime.

"Nice entrance," he commented indolently, eyeing the door to clarify just which entrance he was referring to.

"The same to you," she returned. Karen knew a lot about body language. Judging people with swift precision was necessary in police work. Chandler was deliberately dominating the room, dwarfing the small beige sofa beneath him, filling a good portion of the floor space with his long, lean legs.

He'd come to show her who was boss.

Karen's heavily mascaraed lashes lowered as she envisioned herself pushing him up against a squad car, forcing him into the spread-eagle position for a frisking. The moment of fantasy bloomed swiftly and vividly in her mind, suffusing her with satisfaction.

Ross grimaced as a lazy smile spread across her dramatically made-up face. This meeting wasn't going as planned at all. He'd been expecting a degree of fear, of uncertainty. Offstage, she was proving to be an entirely different woman. Well, perhaps not entirely, he amended. She was still sizzling with sexuality. But now her savvy matched her sizzle.

Didn't these entertainers consider the stage their first home? If so, why did Karen Ford seem more at home in here, far away from the spotlight?

Who was the woman behind the illusion?

More to the point, why was he so fascinated in the first place? Did it really matter? She was a temporary employee. Tiffany would be back at work soon enough. Tiffany, with her feathers and her tantrums and her girlfriends.

An immodest litany of his perquisites as prince of the Pleasure Palace scrolled through his brain as he sought to reassert himself.

He made it a point never to hire anyone he couldn't dominate.

He had a policy against getting personal with the people he did hire.

And when Dinah did the hiring, she normally reflected his policies. But she'd done this blind. Taken on this woman on the word of an old friend. Taken on this spunky, sexy siren with only the barest background for the job!

One look into those liquid blue eyes, those glittering jewels of dangerous energy, and he would've tossed her out on . . . Just what would he toss her out on? He took the excuse of indecision to peruse her length all over again.

Picturing an employee naked, as he was doing now, could prove to be a bad habit. A weakness that could ultimately strip him of his cool. He knew it to be so, because he was already beginning to slide on the slippery satin cushions. His limbs were literally weakening with heat. He had to stop this meltdown before it was too late. Intent on counterattack, he rose to his feet in a quick, fluid motion.

Anticipating his next move, Karen didn't as much as flinch. But his words stung her in a most vulnerable spot.

"I feel I must caution you, Miss Ford," he said, closing in on her. "I'm not sure you're suited for the Starlite Lounge."

The blunt warning set her heart hammering. She tipped up her chin to meet his glare, holding it fast with steady bravado. If he expected to see fear lurking beneath her audaciousness ... Well, there was a good chance his wish would be granted! This was a one-shot deal, her sole opportunity to get close to Wendy. Meet her very own child for the very first time! Her eyes shimmered with need and desperation.

Apparently it was exactly what he'd been looking for.

His brown eyes flinted with triumph as he openly took control of the moment. She would've loved to tell the arrogant bastard that it had nothing to do with his job or his masculine magnetism.

As his look penetrated her as no song ever could, she found her powers of reason diminishing, her clear-cut goals growing just a bit murky around the edges.

Justine's advice about reaching the girl through her father suddenly sprang up out of nowhere. But the realization that no one ever got the better of this man followed like a burning whiskey chaser.

Messing with Ross Chandler on any level would be a dangerous venture. She had done some discreet last-minute checking on the man's professional reputation. He and his brother, Ron, were heavy players not only locally in Nevada but in the south of France, as well. Their Tahoe and Cannes resorts were considered among the most opulent in the world. And their rules the most stringent. Losers promptly paid up. It was just a fact without a whole lot of data behind it. There was nothing treacherous or illegal on record. Nothing she could find with her harried surface search anyway.

She'd come with the hope of keeping passion of any sort out of their encounter. After all, connecting with her daughter for the first time was already tapping deeply into her emotional well. But here she stood, feeling a rush of attraction, of dislike, of frustration with this infuriating macho millionaire. She'd done a fine job of setting a bland tone, of steering them both into vague indifference, she thought with sarcastic self-recrimination.

Oh, how simple this would be if he was still married!

But he was single, on the loose and just the sort of man she was drawn to. Dangerous, cocky, intelligent. And handsome to a fault. Handsome almost to the point of perfection.

And he knew it, damn it! Knew just what sort of power his persona wielded.

But the most urgent issue at hand was that he already had his doubts about her. What an unsettling beginning. With Justine's help, she'd taken great pains to forge a false identity back in Vegas. According to her résumé and certain casino records, Karen Ford had a modest background in singing and just enough experience to match her skills.

She said a silent prayer for leeway. If nothing else, she was jolted into a more cautious mode. The last thing she wanted to do was offend him, goad him into digging deeper for information. If it wasn't too late, she would make an effort to allow him to believe he was in total control.

She cleared her throat, weighing her words carefully in advance. It was an exercise she found unnatural and difficult.

"Mr. Chandler, if you have a complaint about my performance, I'm more than willing to listen. But I am counting on this job. Dinah Delray promised it to me, and I accepted in good faith. It was an inconvenient set of circumstances for me, but it's always been my dream to perform in a place like this, even if only for a week."

"This isn't 'Star Search'!" he chastised. "This is the best. The cream."

"I know that!" she said with strained patience. "But I thought you'd appreciate my swift action. I literally dropped everything for this opportunity. I just up and left my regular position!"

"Not permanently, I hope," he returned tersely.

In other words, *Don't quit your day job.* Karen bristled at his nerve.

Ross stroked the length of his rigid jawline, watching her fingers rake her spray-stiff hair. Her slender hands shook slightly, the sight touching him with a dash of shame. "I just wondered if you understood that you are filling in for a very polished act."

She nodded with a new understanding, all right. He was exercising his ego, making certain that she understood what a huge break this was for her.

"I've got the picture, Mr. Chandler," she replied with a breezy formality.

"I didn't come in here to fire you," he assured her.

No, he came in here to make her squirm. Let her know that she was almost not good enough for his precious Pleasure Palace.

Nerve. Money. Looks.

The dream combination of every single female on the planet.

"I'm sure we'll get along famously," he intoned on a more merciful note, moving toward the door. "If there's anything you want or need . . ."

She watched him pause with his hand on the doorknob. "Yes?" she responded in husky hope.

"Feel free to consult Dinah."

With the sort of smile worthy of a sound slap, he departed.

armers for bacon, hash browns and pancakes. "The
y is blue, the sun is shining—"

"I don't want to go for a hike," she cautioned, reach-
g for her glass of juice. "Miss Walden took us on a
ature walk in gym class on Thursday and I got an itchy
sh on my ankle." When Ross's expression grew pan-
ky, she clicked her tongue and sighed. "Don't worry.
he school nurse gave me some lotion for it. It's almost
one."

"The lotion or the rash?"

"The rash!" she cried in exasperation. When his
eady look didn't waver, she shifted on her chair to
how him her ankle. "See?"

"Yeah." Ross held the heel of her bare foot in his hand
nd examined the inflamed area at her sock line.

"The nurse said there are hundreds of plants on the
ails," she said in dismissal, curling her leg back un-
erneath her.

"I'll be looking at that again tomorrow," he warned.

"I know it," she grumpily agreed.

"I suppose we could go for a hike next Saturday," he
roposed with a teasing twinkle in his eyes.

"On my birthday?" Wendy cried out, aghast.

He set his plate on the table before him, eyeing her
th earnest surprise. "What better way to spend the
y than building up your cardiovascular system while
mmuning with nature?"

You know that the party's almost all planned. I al-
dy sent out invitations and everything."

We'll take the whole crew for a hike!"

No way! You promised supper and a band in the
lite Lounge. You even said you'd leave your porta-
hone here at the house."

ROSS WOKE UP ABOUT NINE the following morning, de-
lighted that it was the weekend, confident that the light
of his life would be waiting for him downstairs.

Despite some blunders in his personal life, he was
wise enough to realize that his daughter, Wendy, was
his lifeline, the spark that made each new day an adventure.

The Pleasure Palace might never again have a reigning queen, but it would have its little princess in Wendy.

No matter how overwhelming the running of the
Pleasure Palace became, Ross was a doting father who
always found time for his bewitching daughter. Crossing paths with her each morning at breakfast was an
essential part of his daily routine—unless he was out
of town on business. During this special time, they
would discuss her school activities, her personal triumphs and concerns. She in turn begged for stories of
his daily encounters with the staff. Many of the resort's employees either lived on site in the hotel or
somewhere nearby, so Wendy viewed them as extended family. Despite his money and powerful position, a stable family unit was one thing Ross couldn't
conjure up for the child. It bruised his ego and his heart.

After their weekday meals, each parted to face the
day ahead. Ross made his morning rounds around the
spacious Palace properties, keeping tabs on the trusted
circle of upper-tier employees who did the hands-on
operating of the resort. More often than not, he then
closed himself away in his suite of offices in the casino
to deal with telephones and paperwork. Wendy was
whisked to a private school several miles away.

Ah, but the weekend time like this was the best, being less structured and more playful. They lingered
longer, sometimes with a guest or an employee. Food

was brought over to their private chalet from the huge commercial kitchen in the main restaurant, or they would sit at their private table in the hotel dining room and people watch.

The best of times for Ross was the time spent with Wendy.

For no matter how the Pleasure Palace glittered with its high energy, excitement and fashionable monied people, the jaded, sophisticated club owner was enraptured with his beautiful, high-spirited child. In a harsh, complicated world, she was his oasis, his jewel, his assurance that real, unconditional love existed.

He wasted no time donning a navy knit shirt and tan pleated shorts and descending the open zigzag staircase of his chalet-style home two steps at a time. The house had been designed as a place to throw fabulous parties, with its three levels and a wall of windows overlooking the Nevada wilderness beyond the flashy resort complex. The ceiling was imported walnut, stretching up to the point of an A-shaped peak. A person could stand on any landing and take in all the action at a glance.

These days, Wendy caused most of the action herself. Few and far between were the private parties for globe-trotting friends. Gone forever were the lavish indulgences Ross had enjoyed before his marriage to Margo. When their union had turned sour, many of his female playmates had called from around the world to see if he was up for some consolation, a rousing reunion. Ross couldn't even imagine such excesses now. With no regrets whatsoever, he turned down all the provocative invitations.

Ross was no monk, but he was the soul of discretion.

Any slipup would make him less than a ther figure. He'd fought hard and long for so of Wendy. Margo hadn't wanted the girl, but her out of spite. With Margo's weaknesse bling and alcohol, he'd managed to convince quietly step aside and relinquish her hold of He'd persuaded her that it would be the bes all of them—and it would keep their family tr of the media. For no matter what had happen marriage, Ross still had some compassio Margo. She was a Chandler. And Ross took own.

Ross found Wendy in the dining room, kn a regal, high-backed chair at the large polish ogling the large array of food that matched th menu offered the guests. An endearing smil ened his flawless face as he approached. The nin old reminded him of a soft, plush bunny. Still in her fluffy pink nightie, she leaned over a through a huge bowl of cut fruit. She was piece of honeydew melon into her mouth as hand covered the top of her blond head.

"Oh, Daddy. Only babies and puppi pats."

"I forgot." With a mock sigh, he slid in ing the wall of windows. The sight of the of mountains in the distance made him Whenever he felt cynical or claustropl perficial merry-go-round world, Ross v backpack and head out into the wilde air and sunshine never failed to clear

"What a beautiful spring Saturda with pleasure as he dug into the s

ROSS WOKE UP ABOUT NINE the following morning, delighted that it was the weekend, confident that the light of his life would be waiting for him downstairs.

Despite some blunders in his personal life, he was wise enough to realize that his daughter, Wendy, was his lifeline, the spark that made each new day an adventure.

The Pleasure Palace might never again have a reigning queen, but it would have its little princess in Wendy.

No matter how overwhelming the running of the Pleasure Palace became, Ross was a doting father who always found time for his bewitching daughter. Crossing paths with her each morning at breakfast was an essential part of his daily routine—unless he was out of town on business. During this special time, they would discuss her school activities, her personal triumphs and concerns. She in turn begged for stories of his daily encounters with the staff. Many of the resort's employees either lived on site in the hotel or somewhere nearby, so Wendy viewed them as extended family. Despite his money and powerful position, a stable family unit was one thing Ross couldn't conjure up for the child. It bruised his ego and his heart.

After their weekday meals, each parted to face the day ahead. Ross made his morning rounds around the spacious Palace properties, keeping tabs on the trusted circle of upper-tier employees who did the hands-on operating of the resort. More often than not, he then closed himself away in his suite of offices in the casino to deal with telephones and paperwork. Wendy was whisked to a private school several miles away.

Ah, but the weekend time like this was the best, being less structured and more playful. They lingered longer, sometimes with a guest or an employee. Food was brought over to their private chalet from the huge commercial kitchen in the main restaurant, or they would sit at their private table in the hotel dining room and people watch.

The best of times for Ross was the time spent with Wendy.

For no matter how the Pleasure Palace glittered with its high energy, excitement and fashionable monied people, the jaded, sophisticated club owner was enraptured with his beautiful, high-spirited child. In a harsh, complicated world, she was his oasis, his jewel, his assurance that real, unconditional love existed.

He wasted no time donning a navy knit shirt and tan pleated shorts and descending the open zigzag staircase of his chalet-style home two steps at a time. The house had been designed as a place to throw fabulous parties, with its three levels and a wall of windows overlooking the Nevada wilderness beyond the flashy resort complex. The ceiling was imported walnut, stretching up to the point of an A-shaped peak. A person could stand on any landing and take in all the action at a glance.

These days, Wendy caused most of the action herself. Few and far between were the private parties for globe-trotting friends. Gone forever were the lavish indulgences Ross had enjoyed before his marriage to Margo. When their union had turned sour, many of his female playmates had called from around the world to see if he was up for some consolation, a rousing reunion. Ross couldn't even imagine such excesses now. With no regrets whatsoever, he turned down all the provocative invitations.

Ross was no monk, but he was the soul of discretion.

Any slipup would make him less than a sterling father figure. He'd fought hard and long for sole custody of Wendy. Margo hadn't wanted the girl, but fought for her out of spite. With Margo's weaknesses for gambling and alcohol, he'd managed to convince Margo to quietly step aside and relinquish her hold on Wendy. He'd persuaded her that it would be the best thing for all of them—and it would keep their family troubles out of the media. For no matter what had happened to their marriage, Ross still had some compassion left for Margo. She was a Chandler. And Ross took care of his own.

Ross found Wendy in the dining room, kneeling on a regal, high-backed chair at the large polished table, ogling the large array of food that matched the brunch menu offered the guests. An endearing smile brightened his flawless face as he approached. The nine-year-old reminded him of a soft, plush bunny. Still dressed in her fluffy pink nightie, she leaned over and picked through a huge bowl of cut fruit. She was pushing a piece of honeydew melon into her mouth as Ross's huge hand covered the top of her blond head.

"Oh, Daddy. Only babies and puppies get head pats."

"I forgot." With a mock sigh, he slid into a chair facing the wall of windows. The sight of the craggy crown of mountains in the distance made him long for a hike. Whenever he felt cynical or claustrophobic in his superficial merry-go-round world, Ross would slip on his backpack and head out into the wilderness. The fresh air and sunshine never failed to clear his head.

"What a beautiful spring Saturday," he announced with pleasure as he dug into the stainless-steel food warmers for bacon, hash browns and pancakes. "The sky is blue, the sun is shining—"

"I don't want to go for a hike," she cautioned, reaching for her glass of juice. "Miss Walden took us on a nature walk in gym class on Thursday and I got an itchy rash on my ankle." When Ross's expression grew panicky, she clicked her tongue and sighed. "Don't worry. The school nurse gave me some lotion for it. It's almost gone."

"The lotion or the rash?"

"The rash!" she cried in exasperation. When his steady look didn't waver, she shifted on her chair to show him her ankle. "See?"

"Yeah." Ross held the heel of her bare foot in his hand and examined the inflamed area at her sock line.

"The nurse said there are hundreds of plants on the trails," she said in dismissal, curling her leg back underneath her.

"I'll be looking at that again tomorrow," he warned.

"I know it," she grumpily agreed.

"I suppose we could go for a hike next Saturday," he proposed with a teasing twinkle in his eyes.

"On my birthday?" Wendy cried out, aghast.

He set his plate on the table before him, eyeing her with earnest surprise. "What better way to spend the day than building up your cardiovascular system while communing with nature?"

"You know that the party's almost all planned. I already sent out invitations and everything."

"We'll take the whole crew for a hike!"

"No way! You promised supper and a band in the Starlite Lounge. You even said you'd leave your portable phone here at the house."

Ross tried to hide his grin from his daughter's yearning, excited scrutiny. "I think it's unfair of you to be so hard on my nature walks and my phone."

She huffed in exasperation. "I am getting too old for all this teasing."

Ross arched a brow in wonder. "Oh? Even the bigger girls around here think I'm hilarious."

"Hey, that's because you're the boss man!"

Ross turned in his chair at the sound of Dinah's cheery voice. The leggy entertainment director was closing in fast over the bright rugs spaced out on the gleaming hardwood floor. She was dressed for a game of tennis in the sort of white cotton outfit he encouraged his employees to wear among the lavishly attired guests.

"Nanny Gee let me in," Dinah explained breezily, taking the few necessary steps up to reach the dining area.

"Join us," Ross invited, aiming his fork at the clean plates stacked at the end of the table.

"Guess I could eat something," she lilted, peeking under the huge silver lids. "Though I've really come over to scold you."

"That job's for Nanny Gee and me," Wendy contributed with a giggle.

"Drink your milk," Ross directed Wendy and settled back in his chair. "So what has this big bad wolf done now?" But he already knew. Knew this had to do with Karen Ford. He was guilty as hell of playing the casino mogul last night in her dressing room. And it wasn't like him to be so damn difficult. He had no choice but to face the music. He didn't want to lose Dinah. And to his surprise, he didn't want to lose Karen, either.

For some crazy reason, he had just wanted Karen's immediate and undivided attention. And her demure adoration. What a pathetic, unexplainable self-revelation!

Dinah sat down opposite him with her plate of food, deliberately obstructing his panoramic view of the majestic mountainside. "Think you overplayed your hand last night?" she asked in a wry chirp, raising two fingers. "Maybe just a little bit?"

He stiffened slightly in his chair. "Well, she's green."

Dinah ran her fingers through her cloud of short red hair. "Ah, a full and prompt confession. More than I hoped for."

"Who's green, Dad?" Wendy asked, eyeing them with interest over the rim of her glass of milk.

"The new singer in the Starlite Lounge," he replied distractedly, always making it a point not to overlook Wendy in a discussion. "She's a bit inexperienced for Tiffany's backup band."

"I spoke to them and they like Karen just fine," Dinah returned sweetly.

"I just wanted to make my opinion known," he stated with a trace of annoyance.

"Were you trying to drive her away?"

"Did I do that?" he asked, jerking forward like a fish caught on a hook.

Dinah's round green eyes glittered mockingly. "No."

"That was a dirty trick," he growled, jabbing a wedge of pancake with his fork.

"Just trying to put you in touch with your own feelings."

"My actions were purely professional," he claimed between bites.

"She got to you," Dinah observed with a smug nod.

"All right, so she's good. In her own way," he clari-fied, pouring Dinah a cup of coffee. "Her own raw, tal-ented way. But I want you to know that I don't care for this kind of blind hiring. A showgirl buddy recom-mends an unknown. You hire her sight unseen. That sort of gamble is better left to the slot machines."

Dinah regarded him sternly over the rim of her bone china cup before taking a sip. "Justine rose through the ranks with me in the early days and I trust her judg-ment as I do my own. Why, she could step in here to-morrow and take over for me."

Ross's mouth twitched. "That's good to know."

"Don't dodge the issue! Karen deserved better from you last night. She rehearsed like crazy yesterday af-ternoon with Tiffany's finicky band—who are de-lighted with her—and then went out there and gave it her best shot. And you know as well as I do that the audience didn't even know the difference between her performance and the more experienced Tiffany Bond's. She drew them in emotionally, sweetie. Everything else is secondary."

"Yeah, well—"

"You know, like life. The emotional trap is always the surest."

Ross arched his most menacing brow. "You think I was taken in? A man who's seen every trick in the book?"

"I know you were taken in," she replied drolly. "I was seated in the lounge not ten feet away from you. I saw you slouched near the exit, panting your little heart out. And it made you so mad that you stormed over to her dressing room to complain."

Dinah had him dead to rights. He was shaken by Karen's ability to seep through his defenses with her music.

"I'm meeting her on the tennis courts in twenty minutes and will relate your apology," Dinah declared with a grin. "Unless I can trust you to do the job."

"Hey, I'd like to meet this one," Wendy declared with an impish look.

"Maybe another—" Dinah attempted to protest as Wendy hopped to her feet, swiping her face with a linen napkin.

"I'll go get dressed. And dig out my racket. Wait for me right here, Dinah!"

# 4

DINAH SHOOK HER HEAD as Wendy scampered up the zigzag staircase leading to her bedroom.

"Do you mind if she tags along?" he asked mildly.

"Not really, Ross. But I think she should ask, not announce." Dinah bit her lip under his distraught look. "You know I love her to pieces, but sooner or later she's got to find out the whole world isn't like this isolated kingdom. Every wish isn't granted with the snap of a finger."

He raised a halting hand. "I'm going to work with her. I admit that Margo's arctic approach to parenting has probably left me overcompensating—"

"Probably?" Dinah clucked dubiously.

"I'm not sure what limits to set yet," he muttered defensively.

"You've been divorced for four years, Ross. Plenty of time for planning new strategies."

"Well, first I had to focus on winning Wendy in court," he offered in excuse. "And, considering how erratic Margo's behavior can be, it seemed most important to reassure her of my love—"

"And now?" she challenged.

"Don't you think that Nanny Gee should be giving her more discipline?" he proposed in an effort to shift the blame. "She's the one who spends the most time with her."

"Nanny Grethal is sixty-eight years old!" Dinah scoffed. "She was your and Ronald's nanny thirty years ago."

"So I know she's made of stern stuff," Ross argued. His father Pearce Chandler had been a prestigious jeweler, who along with his wife, Joan, had been welcome in social circles worldwide. Nanny Gee had been Ross's disciplinarian throughout his formative years. "She knows just how to keep order," he insisted with a vigorous nod. "Why, just one iron look from her would send us running for cover."

"She's evolved right along with you, Ross!" Dinah protested. "You're a father now, and she's blissfully slipped into the doting grandparent role. Haven't you noticed that she's all finished with the fire-and-brimstone bit?"

"Well, no," he slowly denied. "Guess I've been so grateful that she could supply a motherly touch."

"Look, Ross, Wendy is developing into a young lady now. She needs new direction. Firmer direction. She knows everyone around here has to toe the line with you and she's using that clout to run roughshod over us."

"You're blowing this out of proportion," he scoffed.

"Really? I'm sure that's why she wants to join me on the courts," Dinah explained, a dash of apology intermingled with her exasperation. "She's looking for fresh game. Wants to meet Karen Ford and set the tone from the get-go."

Ross's large sensuous mouth settled into a grumpy line. "If this is such a problem, why hasn't anyone complained?"

"At the risk of losing one's job?" she hooted. "Everybody knows how you worship her! And now she's sensed this static with Karen. She's bound to step in and mix things up. Do you think Karen deserves this treatment from both of you?"

"I suppose it would be simpler all around if both Wendy and I kept our distance from Miss Ford for the next week," he decided with a stretch. Yes, it would be wise to forget all about her. She was too green. Too young. Too cocky.

But he didn't want to forget. He closed his eyes for a brief, blissful moment, picturing her on stage. So sensual, so fluid. Hot enough to melt the sequins on her dress.

"What a coward you are!"

Ross's features sharpened as he refocused on his guest across the table. "I just can't please you! What do you want me to do with the woman?"

Dinah gasped. "Ross Chandler, do you have the audacity to sit there and tell me that you don't know what you want to do with her?"

Ross colored slightly under his tan. How could he deny something so obvious to one of his best friends?

"All right, all right. I'll admit I find her interesting," he confessed with effort. "It's been a long while since I've had such an instant reaction to someone. Can't understand it, though. I've seen prettier. And I've seen more cooperative."

Many a singer would've offered her favors last night in the dressing room, been anxious to smooth his ruffled feathers. But not Karen Ford. There was a toughness beneath that sexy shell of hers. True, all show people had a layer of thick skin, but there was something more to her. Her clear blue eyes had mirrored the world somehow, had reflected a wisdom belying her years.

She knew things. She'd seen things. Just when and where was a mystery he was anxious to explore.

Dinah watched the play of emotion on his face with amusement. "You don't even know why you find her so captivating, do you?"

Ross flashed her an annoyed look. "I suppose you do."

Dinah huffed in exasperation. "Think! Isn't there something significant about her qualities?"

His brows narrowed in perplexity. "She's the opposite of Margo in coloring and warmth if that's what you mean."

"For heaven's sake, Ross!" she chided with a laugh. "She is so much like Wendy it's uncanny! She looks like her, moves like her. Even shares her spirit. Don't you see? That's why you were so easily taken in. And it explains why you were so anxious to put the rules out front, to dominate her from the start."

"Oh, c'mon!"

"I just don't want you to miss the crux of your problem or back away because you're bothered by her." Dinah nibbled on a slice of toast with a sly smile. "Think about it, boss. The challenge was there, even before your intellect could identify it. You stormed in on her without even knowing why you were doing it, right? So intent on getting the upper hand before she could wrap you around her—"

"Enough!"

"I am so happy that some lady has finally pierced that armor of yours," she said blissfully. "It's about time you got back in the game with some enthusiasm."

"I am not a love-starved chump."

"Just an overworked one."

Ross lifted a hand in caution. "Look, Dinah, I've just met this lady."

"Sometimes that's all it takes," she blithely retorted. "And I think you've unconsciously been shopping for someone new for a long time. Your instincts reacted before your reason could catch up. You can well afford to step out of your workaholic haze for some exploration."

"Speaking of work," Ross intervened silkily, "I believe you've forgotten about your interview with that troupe of mimes arriving this morning from our French operation."

Dinah clapped her hands to her face. "Oh, damn!"

"You just tend to business today," he lectured, openly enjoying her sheepish pause. "But know, too, that I'm hearing you about Wendy."

"And Karen?" she nervily pressed.

Ross bowed his head to busily butter a slice of toast. Dinah had hit all the targets dead center. Aligned for him all the fragmented facts swirling around in his panic-stricken brain. He did have the hots for Karen in a most basic, uncomfortable way—that age-old mysterious way. The way lightning strikes without warning or reason, leaving a man jolted and burned. And cinder crisp.

Ross hadn't allowed himself to be so totally incinerated by a woman in years. Maybe it was about time he jumped into the fire again. It was against his personal policy to involve himself with female employees. But Karen was, after all, a temporary employee. What possible harm could a bit of flirtation, or even consummation, do either one of them?

"I do want to give this thing with Karen a try," he admitted, openly formulating a plan. "Since Wendy is so anxious to meet her, I'll send her out to the courts to take your place. I'll wander over to watch. If Karen has no interest in either one of us, we'll just pretend we're passing through."

"I wonder if it's wise to lead off with your daughter," Dinah objected. "I suggest that you play it safe, grab the racket and the babe up-front. Sell yourself before you produce Wendy."

"Any woman who is going to involve herself with me will have to accept Wendy, too," he asserted defensively.

Dinah gave a wry smile. "It's a risk at this fragile beginning stage. Young women like Karen dream of daughters who are bundles of joy, not handfuls of spice."

"Oh, c'mon!" Ross flared.

Dinah rolled her eyes. "It will be a miracle if your father-daughter demolition squad doesn't send that much-needed singer packing. A bona fide miracle!"

IT WAS A MIRACLE.

Karen had been out on one of the courts for nearly ten minutes, volleying with a young tennis pro named Chuck, taking some pointers on her overhead strokes.

She appeared out of nowhere, skipping along the path outside the high fence, swinging her tennis racket with ease, claiming the right-of-way as she dodged guests in her path.

It was her baby girl.

It could be no one else with that banner of satin blond hair sailing between her shoulder blades, those lean, lanky limbs tanned to a golden brown like her own. And then there was her nerve—in her step, in the lofty lift of her chin.

...Wendy a ...asn't as sad and lost as Karen had been at that age!

There might be another explanation. Perhaps she was simply spoiled rotten and acting insolently superior in her position as the owner's daughter. She could be as happy as a clam, Karen went on to console herself. Maybe she learned the art of arrogance from her father. In either case, Karen didn't care for Wendy's total disregard for the adults strolling along the walkway.

She wanted to shake some sense into her. But first she wanted to hold her, wanted to touch her face, stroke her hair, squeeze her tight and tell her she just didn't know. Hadn't been given a choice about her fate.

Karen wanted to give her baby all the love in her heart.

But unfortunately she couldn't even tell Wendy that she was her baby.

Joy and panic seized Karen as she realized that Wendy was coming through the chain link gate. Heading her way!

head, meeting the g̲....
Wendy's eyes were slightly darke̲....
her face was a bit narrower. But she had the Bradford
nose, all right, with the bump along the bridge. Karen
had been spared the bump, but both her father and
Irene shared it, as did the generation before them.

"Dinah can't come anymore," Wendy announced
saucily. "She has to work."

"Oh, so you're taking her place then," Karen choked
out. She swallowed hard, hoping to control her con-
tracting throat, give her voice a clearer, more casual
sound.

"It's okay with Dad," Wendy added for Chuck's
benefit.

Chuck obviously recognized a royal dismissal when
he heard one. He said goodbye and hustled over to an
adjoining court to offer his services to a guest practic-
ing her serve.

Karen clutched her racket, peering down at the cool
blond princess dressed in a spotless white tennis suit
similar to her own.

She was close enough to count the freckles on her cheekbones.

Inhale her sweet scent.

The urge to scoop up her child and squeeze her dizzy was unbearably tempting. And it was the very thing she dared not do. Stew had been right, of course. The very idea of Karen entering this situation only for viewing purposes had been risky and impossible.

She was here only to learn and observe. Not to selfishly usurp anyone. She had an ethical obligation to put the girl's best interests first.

It was the brightest—and the toughest—moment of her life. All the emotions Karen had felt over the news that her baby girl had lived were eclipsed by the fresh feelings flooding her system. Her baby was standing before her, all grown up. Healthy, sassy, enchanting.

Karen didn't know whether to laugh or cry. She just knew she didn't dare do either one.

Wendy's Bradford nose crinkled as she studied Karen. Did the child suspect something? Did she know she was adopted? Who'd have expected the resemblance to be so strong? These questions bulleted through Karen's mind with rapid-fire speed.

She took a steadying breath under the girl's scrutiny. "Is anything the matter?"

"Well..." she teased playfully, "you don't look green."

Karen's jaw sagged. "Excuse me?"

"My dad told Dinah you were green on stage, so I just had to come and see for myself."

"Oh, I see." Karen rocked on the heels of her athletic shoes, returning the girl's keen, squinting look. "It just so happens my shade of green burns off in the sunlight."

Wendy was taken aback by the quick comeback. "Hey, that's pretty good."

Karen winked and grinned. "Hey, I've had years of practice. And I'm really not half-bad on stage. I wouldn't have taken the job if I couldn't handle it."

Wendy was visibly impressed with Karen's warm, welcoming demeanor. She stepped closer, eager to share a confidence. "Dinah chewed him out up and down about it. Said you've got the emotion. That's all that really matters, you know," she explained with authority. "Good legs and lots of pizzazz. Heard it a million times around here."

Karen raised her eyes toward the heavens. Irene had to be doing a double backflip over this scenario! Served her aunt right for giving this baby away! Wendy's upbringing would've been so different down in Las Vegas with them. Of course it was natural to feel that she could have done a better job. She clenched her teeth for control. She had to stop dreaming of the shoulda beens! Wendy's present circumstances were what mattered most.

"You sound like a young lady who'd like to be center stage herself someday," she said lightly.

"Oh, no," Wendy scoffed dismissively. "I'm going to run this whole place when I grow up." Under Karen's surprised look, she continued with pleasure. "I'm the only heir so far. We got our divorce and my uncle Ron is single."

Her choice of words was disturbing. Since when did mothers divorce their daughters? "Surely your parents' divorce had nothing to do with you," she dared to venture.

Wendy looked uncertain for the first time. "I make Margo nervous," she confided. "She's just too frickin' young to have a preteen girl," she mimicked with a contorted face.

Karen's pale brows shot up. Margo Chandler had to be thirty-five years old! That sort of vanity seemed disturbingly extreme.

"Of course, Dad makes it all up to me," she hastily assured Karen with a proud, sweeping gesture. "We're a super team. And anybody who wants to be close to my dad has to go through me first. I have a lot of pull around here. For permanent jobs and everything . . ." she said, trailing her words off craftily.

"So you're the girl to know, eh?"

Wendy's eyes twinkled with pride.

"I'm afraid I don't want a permanent job here," Karen informed her teasingly with a twinge of regret.

"You don't?" Wendy asked in disbelief and disappointment.

"Nope. But I still think we could be friends."

"Don't you even care about what I can do for you? Get you in good with my dad?"

Karen bent over to meet her incredulous face squarely. "No."

"But everybody else—"

"I'm not like everybody else," Karen interrupted, pinching her chin.

"But everybody wants something," Wendy protested with a suspicious squint.

"Not me. I'm independent. I like who I like. And I like you just because you're you."

"Never happened around here before. . . ." Wendy muttered doubtfully.

"I bet Dinah likes you."

Wendy shrugged her slim shoulders. "Yeah, maybe her. Oh . . ." she said, making a frustrated noise, "Let's just play some tennis!"

"Okay."

"I'm gonna tromp ya," Wendy announced with a cocky grin.

"Oh, no, you aren't," Karen heartily declared, anxious to gain some ground with the overly confident youngster. She went over to collect some bright orange tennis balls from a box near the gate and trotted back with a sure step. "I may be green on stage, but out here on the courts, I'm dynamite!"

Karen's veins were pumping pure adrenaline as she tossed a ball into the air and caught it. She simply had to burn off some of her nervous energy! The girl was shrewd, sharp as a tack. She would suspect Karen was up to something if she didn't calm down.

Karen stepped behind the service line watching Wendy position herself in the receiver position with practiced body movements. Undoubtedly she played a lot. But so did Karen. Every week with Judge Stewart. Karen tossed the ball in the air, and with a good snap of her wrist, smacked the ball with her racket, bulleting it over the net. Wendy had underestimated her prowess and was unable to capture the ball before it rolled out of play.

"Fifteen-love!" Karen called out before serving all over again. Love. She wanted to shout it into the brilliant blue skies above! Karen went on to tromp her daughter in a series of games, shouting out love over and over again. She felt light-headed, crazy and pleased. She'd actually done it. She'd moved in on her own little girl. And she'd done it without arousing anyone's suspicion.

Sometime during the set, Ross had wandered into the outdoor café located right outside the chain-link fencing. He sat down at one of the round wrought-iron tables with a tall glass of iced tea. He watched with interest, marveling at the pair, huffing and charging their way around the court.

The lovely blondes could've passed for sisters. Dinah had been right about that source of his enchantment. But she had been wrong about Wendy's lack of diplomatic skills. The pair was obviously having a good time. Wendy hadn't driven Karen off bag and baggage. It was a nice scene. Relaxing and nice.

With his long, hair-dusted legs crossed at the ankle, Ross took his regular amount of invasive Sunday-morning calls on the wallet-size portable phone he kept clipped to his belt. Ross spoke to members of his staff from all corners of the resort, from the casino floor to the hotel's front desk.

All the while, Wendy was in good hands. He could sense that from a hundred yards away. Karen had a competent backhand grip found only on the strongest players. Ross winced more than once as Wendy fumbled with squeals of frustration. Karen didn't ease up on her as he would have—as apparently his regular employees would have—but stopped the game at regular intervals to circle the net and show Wendy the right way to swing her racket.

As the games stacked up in her favor, Karen dwelled on the most important losses. She and Irene could have raised this child! Between the two of them, they could've given her a home. If Karen had known, had the option, she would've worked harder, earned more money.

But she hadn't known. Wasn't given the chance to make a choice. Instead she'd mourned her baby's death year after year. Nine times she'd endured the loss. Nine stinkin' times, right under Irene's nose!

As Wendy turned to retrieve the ball for a serve, Karen turned to wipe the sheen of perspiration from her face. There were tears on her cheeks, as well. Tears of jubilation, and frustration. She swiped her jawline with the back of her hand, struggling with her internal world of secrets.

Then something made her jerk her head up with a start. Ross Chandler was standing there hovering over her.

His gaze was as penetrating as a soothsayer's. Thank heavens he couldn't really read her mind! Her thoughts would rock the gleam from his face but fast!

"In the habit of monitoring your new employees day and night, Mr. Chandler?" she saucily demanded, hoping to set a lighter tone between them.

"Only the ones with the smoothest strokes," he returned on a velvet tongue. "And I wish you'd call me Ross."

"Might make it awkward," she objected, easily reading the interest in his eyes. "Confuse our positions."

"Might be awkward if you didn't. All my employees call me Ross." He took a step closer, his mouth quirking with mischief. "And believe me, I've yet to find myself confused in any position. No matter how precarious."

Karen gulped under his attentive gaze. Good lord! He was hitting on her! She hadn't expected him to actually do that!

You certainly came highly recommended to Di-
[n]," he commented, stretching back in his chair. "An
[d] friend you share?"

It was a leading question if she'd ever heard one. But
[K]aren kept her body loose as she rested her forearms
[o]n the table. His was a gracious inquiry, not a grilling
[o]ne.

"Yes," she replied brightly. "Justine Wilson. Apparently she and Dinah go way back."

"You mentioned last night that you had a regular
job," he remarked expectantly.

"Yes." She swallowed hard. This was quite a dilemma. She wanted to know this man better, be up-
front with him about as much as possible. "I work for
the county. Social work. Clerical reports. That kind of
thing."

"Not all people can adjust to the late hours of an entertainer," he marveled.

"I work rather crazy hours as a rule," she explained
breathlessly.

"Few people can leave their jobs, their lives, so
abruptly," he pressed on.

"Well, I was in line for a vacation. And I'm single, so
I had no one to answer to." She smiled to give her explanation the lightest weight. "Just come and go as I
please."

"I have very deep roots here," he explained, giving
Wendy's hand a squeeze. "Of course, I sometimes fly
to our sister resort in Cannes, but the trips are short. I
feel my daughter needs a stable base."

He was really trying to be the best kind of father.
Karen's heart squeezed as he slid the girl a wink. Talk
about drawing on emotions. He was pushing all her
buttons without singing a note. And those eyes . . . Hot

So last night's confrontation had been some sort of
mating call.

The thought had entered her mind later on in bed, as
she struggled to simmer down for sleep. His reaction to
her had been so dramatic. She'd gotten to him on some
level. Apparently it had been an emotional one. Karen
knew that a good ballad singer tugged at a listener's
heartstrings, often forcing feelings to the surface.
Wendy had said he'd keyed in on that strong point in
her act.

Karen regarded him with a new measure of understanding. She'd pushed some of his internal buttons and
it had jolted him.

Well, well, beneath his lord-of-the-manor attitude,
he'd been attracted to her all the while. He just hadn't
known how to express himself. Apparently he was
giving it another shot.

But this guy was high-voltage trouble. Just the kind
of carelessly arrogant personality that she was so drawn
to over and over again. The kind of reckless guy who
admired her police work and understood the thrills of
risk-taking.

But she'd come to spy. Stand in judgment on her
child's adoptive parent.

One hard, assessing look into his glittering eyes told
her that he was already mentally making love to her.

And he knew she knew.

Sharing that shocking realization with him, without
even touching him, sent a sensual quiver down her
sweat-slicked spine. And gave her the courage to return fire.

"What's the matter, Ross?" she lilted huskily.
"Haven't you ever seen green in the light of day before?"

Red proved to be his color of the day. He actually had the grace to blush slightly beneath his dark tan. He promptly turned to regard his turncoat daughter, now inching away from his left elbow. "Wendy..."

"Gee, Dad, I didn't know it was a secret. You were shouting it before."

Ross bared even white teeth as he regarded one nymph, then the other. He was caught in his own trap. "Guess I overdid the ranting a bit."

Wendy erupted in a squealing sound. "Wow, does he like you!"

"Wendy..." Ross halfheartedly cautioned.

She wasn't listening. She was too busy marveling at Karen with an ever-growing respect. "He usually doesn't let his employees get away with diddlysquat!" she confided confidentially.

"Care to join us for a drink?" he offered, tapping a finger on his daughter's lips.

Karen accepted with a nod.

The trio strolled over to the whitewashed café where Ross had been watching their match. They settled into chairs at the end table topped with a red umbrella. Karen requested an ice tea, and Wendy a lemonade.

"So you were here all the time," Wendy said, noting his sunglasses and half-empty glass on the wrought-iron tabletop.

"Some of the time," he replied. "You were looking good."

Wendy let out a long sigh. "Dad, maybe you can explain to Karen about how I win a lot around here. Everybody understands," she added meaningfully.

"Life is full of disappointments, kiddo," Karen automatically observed with a buffering lilt to her tone.

But it wasn't enough to pacify [...] wrinkled in discontent.

Karen could see the internal struggle [...] her. She obviously liked Karen, but wa[...] into her own comfortable reality. Thou[...] that she herself had taken far too many kn[...] her own youth, she knew that a certain a[...] necessary for growth. The real world woul[...] ing for Wendy, no matter how sheltered her ch[...]

She turned to Ross to gauge his reaction to [...] mark. To her annoyance, a trace of a grimace [...] his strong tanned features before he smiled a[...] Surely he didn't want Wendy to expect a victory [...] every move? But it apparently stacked up that w[...] seemed to be the tone set here at the resort. Karen had[...] misinterpreted Wendy's regal, superior attitude. She [...] be naive to think anything else. Karen shook her head [...] with an inward lament. Ross, oh, Ross, what kind of [...] gilded cocoon have you wrapped this little girl in anyway?

Wendy was still grumbling her case when she shook off her reverie. Ross seemed to be struggling with a [...] ply.

"Honey, maybe you should just concentrate [...] beating Karen the next time," he eventually suggest[...] "She gave you a lot of tips. Use them to knock her so[...] off."

Wendy's face brightened. "Yeah. I'll do that!"

"And the win will be sweeter because it's fair [...] square," Karen couldn't help chiming in, ruffling [...] girl's golden mane.

Their drinks arrived. The sun-drenched tennis p[...] ers downed theirs with a deep thirst. Ross left hi[...] touched as he studied Karen with open interest.

liquid brown. Steaming with sensuality. He was focusing on her again with open interest and a bit of foxy intent. There was so much mirrored in his look. It made fascinating reading.

First and foremost, Karen felt that Ross Chandler had a huge capacity for loving. Different kinds of love to different kinds of girls.

Karen slumped a little in her cool iron chair as a quivering tingle raced along her spine. She was swiftly developing a crush on this guy.

They shared a long intimate look while Wendy chattered on to the waitress about her ever-improving tennis game.

"Maybe we should give Karen the grand tour," Ross proposed suddenly, bringing instant affirmation from Wendy. "Would you like that, Karen?"

Karen's smile curved with open pleasure under his hopeful gaze. "That would be nice. Very nice."

Ross led them to a parking lot behind the café, where a half-dozen white golf carts with candy-striped canvas roofs were lined up for guest convenience. He paused to speak to the attendant in the little service hut set off on the grass and came back with a key ring hooked to his finger. He helped Wendy into the back seat and Karen into the front, then eased behind the wheel.

Ross played guide as well as driver as they rolled down the spotless ribbons of curving blacktop. There was no boasting edge to his tone as he named points of interest. His mission was to inform rather than impress. The resort was twelve hundred acres, he reported over the purr of the engine. He'd built it up to this sumptuous point gradually over the years with the help of his older brother, Ronald. Karen took in the plush eighteen-hole golf course and the pool area with its whirlpools and sun decks. The grounds spread out expansively. Most of the buildings were low and self-contained, blending in with the rolling scenery. There was a natural feel throughout, with pine trees and bright cheery flower beds planted along the sidewalks and streets. Ross explained that the hotel building where she was staying was obviously the highest, positioned just right to give its guests a panoramic view from all sides.

Karen drank it all in with wide-eyed wonder, doubting that there was a less-than-perfect view from any angle. The place was pure magic. A small, exclusive colony nestled in natural glory, where the land was as rich as the casino wealth that sat upon it.

Clear alpine waters, a cloak of majestic mountains. The ambiance was almost too perfect, too theatrical to be real.

No wonder Wendy was having a hard time adjusting to life's tougher realities.

There had to be a reason why Ross was going overboard in structuring her world into a Disney-like fantasy. She wanted desperately to understand. But time was so limited. She had one single week to play the fretful, caring mother from afar.

They rolled on, laughing and talking and having fun. Karen listened to their every exchange like a starving urchin, envious, but impressed with their closeness, their easy rapport. How cozy it must feel to be so immersed in a loved one's world. She'd never shared that sort of easy intimacy with Irene or a lover.

The phone hooked to Ross's belt began to bleep just as they were pausing at a crosswalk. "I'm surprised we've had this much peace," he told Karen on an apologetic note as he pulled over to the curb. He shifted into park and swiftly unfolded the flat instrument, pulling up its small antenna before raising it to his ear.

"Ross here." He listened intently, his jaw tightening. "She's on the floor now? All right. Yeah. Not another cent of credit. I'll be right over." He pressed his thumb over the disconnect button and gazed back at his daughter for a long, thoughtful moment.

"You have to go, don't you?" Wendy demanded, her lower lip jutting out in disappointment.

Ross shifted on the seat and set a large hand on Wendy's skinny knee. "Baby, your mother's here."

"Not now!" Wendy cried out in surprise. "She just can't be, Dad!"

"I'm going to speak with her in my office. I want you to come along—"

"She can't see me like this!" Wendy shrieked, slapping her hands to her cheeks in horror. "I'm not good enough!"

Karen clenched her fists in her lap, vibrating with rage. This display was due to the simple appearance of Margo Chandler? She closed her eyes for a brief, agonizing moment. How could the anxious adoptive mother of long ago have turned into such a despised monster? Wendy was terrified. No wonder Ross had sole custody!

"That's nonsense, Wendy," Ross chided gently.

"I have to do my hair, take a bath, get perfect!" she babbled brokenly. "You know that, Daddy, you know that!"

"Oh, Wendy," Karen cooed in sympathy, turning to reach back and squeeze the girl's hand. "You look lovely just as you are."

"She's right, honey." Ross's tone was sincere, but his gaze skittered around as he wrestled internally with a dose of uncharacteristic helplessness. Karen realized that he was openly embarrassed by the display and all it revealed about his ex-wife. And she knew her expression of horror wasn't going to soothe him, but she couldn't help it.

Karen was absolutely floored by the child's metamorphosis. She'd shifted from perky petulance to utter devastation. On the outside she was the spoiled daughter of the boss, but on the inside she was spoiled in a more heartbreaking way.

Wendy was the princess of the Pleasure Palace, but it was surely secondary in her mind to being the quivering daughter of Margo Chandler. Ross's motivation was swiftly coming into clear focus. He was working at damage control. Wendy was as fragile as crystal. A small, wounded lamb in the self-esteem department.

Given this new insight, Karen felt she understood Wendy far more clearly than anyone else on earth possibly could. She was a carbon copy of Karen at that age, sharing the same sassy attitude. But it was a protective shield, nothing more. A means to fend off further pain.

Ross opened his arms to embrace the girl as she bounced forward in her seat. He kissed her forehead and swept his thumbs over her tear-stained face.

"Now I'm blotchy, too," she squeaked with a sniff.

"Maybe it would help if I took her back to your house first," Karen offered, struggling with her composure. "She could clean up and calm down."

Ross frowned. "But if she just hurried and got it over with—"

"You don't understand, Dad!" Wendy wailed, sending a frantic look to Karen.

"I'm doing my best," he said bleakly.

"Ross, perhaps this is a thing just between the girls," Karen suggested with a smooth firmness.

"Oh, please, Dad," Wendy begged, clasping her hands. "Karen knows what I mean, better than you do. I just can't—I just don't want to be wrong."

"Whatever makes you happy, honey," Ross murmured, shooting Karen a grateful look. "It would be nice of you to help her through this, Karen. I'd really owe you."

"No, you wouldn't," Wendy objected, pushing her wind-rippled hair out of her vision. "Karen is my friend, too. She wants to help me."

"Of course I do," Karen assured her, patting the girl's slender, sunbaked arm.

"I'll just walk over to the casino," Ross decided, easing out of the cart. "You can drive Wendy back to the house. She'll show you the way."

Karen rounded the vehicle to slip behind the wheel. Wendy climbed up beside her.

"Do I really have to see her, Dad?" she called out in a last-ditch effort, blinking her moist eyes.

Ross sighed heavily, clearly uncomfortable. "I'll try to steer her clear, honey. But she has a legal right to visit."

"It'll be all right," Karen affirmed. With a nod to Ross, she pulled away from the curb.

Ross watched them take the next corner to loop back to the chalet, then began his journey on foot. He would use the time to calm down, to think. This situation with Margo had gone from bad to worse, no question about it. She had bi-weekly visitation rights, but she seldom used them. He'd been annoyed in the beginning, but recently he'd felt nothing but relief. Her treatment of

Wendy had developed into something intolerable. At first treating their daughter with cool indifference had been bad enough, but now that Wendy was maturing into young adulthood, Margo seemed threatened by her—as she was by all females. She seemed on a campaign to keep the girl insecure. Her visits of the past several months had been supercharged with a new tension even more unworthy of her.

But she kept coming back for more, intent on dipping into his heart and his wallet. But he was going to put a stop to it, he decided abruptly. Karen's shock and disapproval were just what he needed. There was no reason on earth why they had to humor Margo any longer. As deep as his family loyalty ran, as much as he hated failing anyone, he just had to sever the ties.

Karen Ford was like a ray of sunshine in his clouded, hazy existence. His initial fascination with her had been prophetic. She was candid and compassionate—something he found lacking in many of the cloying women who tried to infiltrate his monied life-style. And she was interested in him and Wendy as a package. That had never happened once since his divorce. Several of his dates had shown a tolerance for his child. But not a real interest, not a real kinship.

She almost seemed to like Wendy a bit more than him.

He'd sensed an instant camaraderie between the pair at the first scent of trouble. They'd flatly shut him out there for a minute, drawn an unmistakable line between the sexes! It was the first time he'd ever felt left out of Wendy's world, for sadly and remarkably, Margo had never accomplished that feat with her own daughter. He was a little annoyed, a little confused . . . and a little pleased. Wendy needed it. It was just the kind of thing Dinah had been telling him was missing from her life.

Ross moved a bit faster, with a new spring in his already-determined step. For the first time in a long time, Ross was dreaming again of romantic possibilities for himself, even daring to indulge in whimsical thoughts of second chances.

# 5

ROSS CONSIDERED the Sultan's Room the nerve center of the Pleasure Palace. It was the focal point always featured in magazine layouts. It was on the cover of the Palace's own brochures. The grandiose casino had been constructed with deliberate panache, ballroom-size and -style, with a high ceiling and huge crystal teardrop-shaped chandeliers. Red and black were the predominant colors while gold was the accessory. Almost everything was gilded, from the fixtures to the foil wallpaper.

An opulent playground, where the superrich and the average tourist rubbed shoulders every hour of every day.

A timeless, windowless hideaway, where millions could be won and lost in a matter of minutes.

A fantasy world, self-contained and self-absorbed.

It was the ideal setting for Margo Payne Chandler.

Like the casino, she, too, was obviously overdone. Her surface shell was aglitter with a striking beauty and extravagant attire. She blended into the scenery with chameleon grace.

Ross stood at the double-door entrance for a few moments, scanning the energized room for his ex-wife. Yes, the room fit Margo like a glove. It was a sad irony that this was the worst environment for her. Margo was tragically addicted to gambling. An impetuous woman, who could drop a bundle of cash in a heartbeat, a

Not that it really mattered. Margo was a slave to the impulsion. The winning and losing were secondary the risk itself.

But she did enjoy winning in all things. Margo eedily added the new chips to her stack. Before she uld stop him, Ross had reached down and scooped e smooth, flat disks into his large hand.

"What are you doing?" she demanded.

"Collecting your toys. Playtime's over."

"But I'm ahead of the game," she protested, her voice ow loud and sharp for all to hear.

"Only a temporary condition," he drawled dryly, ssisting her to her feet. With graceful force, he steered er up the carpeted ramp and out of the pit. His fingers vere curled tight around her forearm as he guided her hrough the milling gamblers.

The casino's offices were located in the back of the uilding on a level above all the action, accessible by levator or staircase. Ross decided the exercise would o his ex-wife good and marched her past the security uard keeping vigil on the lavish bank of spiral steps. hough irate over his interruption, Margo still en- ved Ross's touch. The fingers digging into her arm eath the rich fabric of her sleeve, the way his thigh shed hers as they ascended the stairs. There was a gnizable smugness banked beneath her discon-

ss was aware of all of Margo's desires. She was ulsively covetous in all her vices. It had been ages he'd felt anything but a lingering pity for her. Years miliarity had tarnished her brassy shine in his The unthinkable had eventually happened. He her dull.

childish woman, who would then pout because she had no funds to support her opulent life-style.

Ross never did feel responsible for her problems. He was certain that she'd be a betting woman no matter what her environment. Gambling was everywhere, down at a neighborhood bingo parlor, out at the race- tracks. She would wager on the weather if given the chance. But in his capacity as a casino owner, he did feel something like the bartender husband serving drinks under the nose of an alcoholic wife. During their mar- riage, he'd felt obligated to make abstinence easier. He'd contacted the most renowned specialists, even pur- chased another home in Malibu, where she could still function as queen bee with all her social contacts.

But Margo denied her affliction and had no desire to help herself by accepting his help. When he'd assumed her to be happy and content across the California bor- der, she'd been sneaking back to Las Vegas, racking up major tabs down there.

That had been the final straw. That was when he'd filed for divorce.

Ross had been doing his level best to continue doing the right thing by her, despite their bitter breakup. He'd extended her cash way beyond her alimony payments, offered a sympathetic ear to her trials and tribulations.

All he'd asked of her in return was that when she checked in with Wendy she express an interest in her child and make some desperately needed motherly overtures.

She'd made an effort in the beginning, calling from Malibu, commuting from her Las Vegas apartment. But she just wasn't cut out for the role. Her failures with Wendy frustrated her and she'd backed off almost al- together, zooming in on occasion to stir things up—like today. For Margo to be forgotten altogether, to be dismissed like yesterday's news, was the ultimate insult.

Ross understood the background that had formed her troubled personality. A Boston blue blood from the politically influential Payne family, she had been groomed from girlhood for a life of privilege. Image was everything to the Paynes. Unhappily their fortunes weren't quite as stable as their snobbish reputation.

Marrying into the wealthy Chandler clan had given Margo the financial boost she'd always dreamed of. But it was never enough. She'd drain him dry given half the chance.

But far more importantly, she was draining Wendy emotionally. He could well afford the cash, but Wendy's self-esteem could not afford the assaults. The divorce had been final for over four years now, and they were still running through the same old cycle.

It was going to end without further delay.

Seeing Karen's reaction to Wendy's discomfort drove home the dilemma with new insightful force. Controlling Wendy's exposure to her mother, making certain that he was always present, wasn't the way. He'd humored Margo long enough. One way or another, he had to cut her loose.

Money was the answer.

And he didn't mean a payoff. She'd only gamble it away and storm back at them. No, he would have to cut her off. Supply her alimony and nothing more.

Fueled with new purpose, he began to move through the crowded, noisy room with the easy grace of a titled lord, past the rows of slot machines, around the blackjack and craps tables. A disarming smile split his handsome face as he played the goodwill ambassador,

offering cordial hellos to his regulars, wink
luting his dealers. He loved his carnival.
proper perspective, it was the ultimate sho
ticated fun for the reckless and adventurou

He eventually tracked down Margo in th
pit, seated at one of the felt-covered table
cards out of the shoe. A spectator's game a
namental woman had drawn a crowd to t
ropes around the pit. Margo had to be in her
of heaven. On display for admiring eyes,
dressed in a peacock blue pantsuit and sapp
rings. The suit was Armani and the gemsto
Cartier. He had the itemized bills in his office
it.

Margo spared Ross only a cursory look as
fell on her shoulder. "Those little spies of yo
quick on their toes," she greeted in a low, even to
smile frozen for audience effect. Still youthful
five, she looked radiant, with her short cap
black hair, deep blue eyes and expressive m

"If you could give me a moment of your t
toned in a steely but softly modulated voi

"Patience, darling," she said in airy dis

She studied the two cards in her hand
It was a natural win at a total of nine. H
lied the dollar worth of the chips stacke
was ahead of the thousand-dollar cre
The croupier, a young man in hi
dressed in the Sultan Room's unifo
black slacks and red bow tie, sent
nificant look across the table.

Margo was on a bona fide win

The staircase led to a single door on a decorative balcony. Behind it was housed a powerhouse security system, which not only kept vigil on the games below, but had the capacity to monitor all the zones of the resort.

The small decorative door popped open as they approached. Ross whisked her inside, dropping his hand from her arm.

Out of the public eye, Margo's moves were far less theatrical. She perused the group of sober-looking personnel manning the computers and television monitors. "Hello, David," she called out in drippy sweetness. "Still looking out for me, I see."

The stout, balding man nodded with a glimmer of amusement. "Your presence is never overlooked for long."

"Rat." With a huff, she glided back toward Ross's corner office.

Ross followed her inside his large paneled sanctuary, closing the door firmly behind him. The space was soundproofed, and the sudden silence between them was deafening. It was just this kind of quiet moment away from the glitter that had driven home their mutual disinterest in each other as loving partners. Four and a half years ago, they had sat down in this very office to discuss the debts Margo had accrued down along the Vegas strip. He'd begged her, for the sake of their family, to seek help for her gambling problem.

It had been shameful for him to admit, but after all those years of a jet-set marriage, it was the first time they'd slowed down enough to take a good long look at each other. Her troubling behavior had been quite a reality jolt. Up-front conversation, blunt communication were both long overdue. It was within a short span of time, however, that they realized it just wasn't going to happen. Mr. and Mrs. Chandler were not about to conquer their shortcomings as a couple united against the world. Isolation time together was like doing prison time. Without the party-circuit crowd to decorate their world, they stood alone with nothing.

The bottom line had been that Margo refused to give an inch. She perceived herself as a master of self-control, the author of her own fate. She didn't have a problem with excess. All the friends in her social circle enjoyed gambling and alcohol. It was acceptably chic.

So in the end, Margo sacrificed their marriage and her mother-daughter relationship for the sake of her feckless life-style.

But the divorce and the total collapse of their physical relations weren't about to discourage Margo from flirting even now. She'd shifted into a seductive slouch in her chair, one leg crossed over the other, and she was wearing the scent that he'd always liked best.

The blatant play for a sexual response irritated him more than usual this time, with Wendy's panicky spectacle still playing in his head. And that extra annoying nudge was good for him. It gave him the urge to deal with Margo with the sort of autocratic bluntness she deserved.

He edged his hip over the front of his large oak desk, hovering beside her chair with a glance at the silver watch on his wrist. "Not like you, to be out past your noon-hour bedtime."

"You know I don't like routine, darling." Under his expectant look, she removed an engraved gold case from her purse and pried it open with long manicured fingernails. It contained a neat row of slim black cigarettes.

"Foreign?" he queried with interest.

"Yes, but you didn't pay for them," she promptly assured him. "They're a gift from an Arab oilman. Quite good really. Care for one?"

"All right."

Ross set two cigarettes between his lips and lit them with his desktop lighter. He took a drag, then handed one to Margo. He noted with a trace of surprise that her hand was shaking slightly. They smoked together for a long pensive moment, studying each other in the gathering haze. Gauging, wondering, second-guessing.

"So just how do I merit a visit, Mar?" he asked with a benign smile. "There must be something you want."

She lifted a thin black brow. "Am I really that transparent?"

He shrugged. "Consistent is a better choice of words."

She bristled at his unflattering response. "Does it really make a damn bit of difference either way?"

Not a damn bit to him. "Just trying to be polite," he intoned.

"Oh, yes," she oozed smartly. "The unflappable sultan in his shiny palace. Civilities are so important."

To the contrary, he was feeling more and more uncivilized by the moment. But this was the destined course for their encounters. They always started with the social amenities, soon falling to a down-and-dirty level. More than ever before, he wanted to put these visits, these verbal duels behind him forever. But he fought to temper his emotions, keep his shield in place. Margo was so good at penetrating a weak area. And Wendy was his weakest. He had to land on top today. Make his points and make them stick. "Short on funds?" he inquired silkily.

"The usual budgeting problems," she admitted with an accusatory note.

"I haven't had a call from the bank in hours," he drawled mockingly.

"I'm in no mood for a penny-pinching lecture today, Ross."

His mouth stretched to a slit of a smile. "You wouldn't know a penny if it pinched your bottom, Margo."

She gasped indignantly. "Well, thank you very much! With the allotment I've been getting, I can damn well assure you I know about pennies."

"Liar." Twin streams of smoke poured from his nostrils as he stubbed out the remains of his cigarette in the ashtray beside him. He allowed himself an inward grunt of satisfaction. She'd walked right into his snare with her petty whining. It was time to yank away the perks.

"How dare you treat me this way, you arrogant bastard of a man." She sputtered then suddenly lunged out at him with her glowing cigarette. He snared her wrist and forced her to grind out the butt beside his in the ashtray.

"You win, Margo. There will be no more lectures on money," he vowed on a growl as she wrenched free, reeling back into her chair. "You will be in control of your own budget from now on."

She huffily smoothed her Armani suit. "So what's the catch?"

His white teeth were bared against his tan skin. "I am withdrawing all my financial support above and beyond your rightful alimony payments."

"You're joking!" she screeched, clenching her fists. "That's brutal! Unthinkable!"

"I feel like we've been chasing around in circles ever since the divorce," he continued on sternly, his strong, wiry arms primed to fend off any further attack. "At first it was a few extra dollars here and there for one bauble or another. But a disturbing pattern has formed. You've come to rely too heavily on that extra income."

Her eyes narrowed to slits. "I need that money to keep up with my circle of acquaintances!"

"You could support a small country on your legal allowance," he thundered back, pounding his desktop with a mighty fist. "If it was spent with even the minimum of responsibility."

"I have a life-style!"

"You have an addiction!" he countered, leaning forward and crowding her back in her chair. "A habit so destructive that it cost you a share in Wendy's custody."

"You're so damn proud of that victory, aren't you?" she hissed in his face.

"She isn't a victory, Margo. She's a little girl who needs a mother."

"You've certainly wasted no time in turning her totally against me," she accused him fiercely.

Quite the contrary was true. Ross had been trying all along to smooth over Margo's sharp edges in an effort to heighten the girl's self-esteem. But Margo couldn't even begin to understand the complexities behind his motivation. Brittle, abrasive, self-absorbed, Margo was sensitive only to her own spa-pampered hide.

It was a heartbreaking situation watching a little girl yearn for a loving mother and battling internally with relief and despair as that mother kept her distance. Whenever Ross managed to soften Margo's sharper edges in Wendy's perception, Margo inevitably showed up to drive home the harsher truths. Margo had been jealous over his easy rapport with the child ever since the beginning. A stable, caring mother would only want to enhance such a relationship, join in and make the bond a three-sided affair. It had been his dream for far too long that Margo could reshape her character, transform into the sort of caregiving role model every husband and child yearned for.

Well, on this sunny Saturday in May, the dream was finally struck dead.

They'd had these face-offs so many times before. But visions of Karen Ford delighting in his daughter for no gain of her own danced in his head today, making this family triangle seem so much uglier, so much more intolerable.

There was more to life out there. He owed it to himself and to Wendy to clear the way.

"I've done my best to assure Wendy that you love her in your own fashion," he informed Margo in stiff honesty.

"Now you're the liar!" she cried in accusation.

"This is just no good for any of us!"

"You can't even deny it," she ranted on. "Wendy's loyalties are completely with you."

"A competent mother would be lobbying for love first and foremost," he lectured in disgust. "What's this loyalty bull mean to a little girl?" He matched her tight-lipped glare. "Do you realize you haven't been in touch with her for over three months? What gives you the right to storm in here raving on about anything!"

"It hasn't been that—"

"It has." He pinched her chin as she tried to turn away. "Do us all a favor and go home. To Boston. To your family. Remove yourself from the temptations here, Margo, and try to put your life back together."

"I'm afraid that wouldn't be such a good idea right now," she argued, her hot, minty breath only inches from his face.

"Why not?"

She pushed his hand from her face with a sniff. "Because I'm in some trouble, down in Vegas."

The scowl on his dark features deepened. "What kind of trouble?"

"I didn't do anything," she replied defensively. "It's just . . . some of the owners think . . ."

He caught his breath. "They don't suspect you of being involved in that counterfeit-chip disaster?" One look into her petulant face told him it was so.

"I'm not passing those chips," she babbled in a strangled voice as his hands closed around her shoulders. "I'm not involved at all!"

"But you've been running with the people who are," he surmised grimly.

"I suppose. I've heard snatches of things, but I really don't have any proof."

"The wrong men will always drag you down along with them."

"But they seemed so right at first," she offered in defense. "Powerful, monied—"

"Nobody knows your needs better than me," he grated.

"Fix it for me, Ross," she pleaded, fluttering her heavy black lashes. "Tell the police, the casino security, whoever's involved, that you know I'm not guilty!"

He yanked her up. "Look at me and tell me you're innocent."

"I am!" she wailed.

Most likely she was telling the truth. He'd never seen naked fear in her eyes before. "People will be going to prison over this—"

"I know!" She pressed her hands over his chest. "Think of how it will tarnish you, too," she babbled on, slyly drawing him into the fray. "Helping me will help save your own reputation as an honest casino owner."

Ross's jaw compressed. What a mercenary bargaining tactic. If only she had tried to appeal to his more gallant nature, the soft spot that had been fueling his compassion all this time. But she was incorrigible.

"I'll do what I can," he promised, abruptly releasing her.

She picked up her discarded purse. "I believe I'd like to see Wendy now."

"Maybe it would be better if you bypassed that visit today, considering the state you're in."

"I have a legal right to see her," she snapped back in true form. "And I will see her!"

"Interesting how some legalities concern you more than others."

She made a doubtful, snorting noise. "Is she at the house?"

"Yes, but—"

"I'll just go over there."

"I'll drive you over in one of the carts." With quick strides, he joined her at the door.

"The great sultan making time to appear on the home front in the afternoon?" she taunted in surprise. "That doesn't sound like the absentee husband I knew."

Ross silently mused that Wendy had managed to domesticate him in ways Margo would have found unthinkable. Everything from washing worthless rocks for her costume-jewelry hobby kit, to in-line skating down at the local rink.

"Mightn't this bore the living hell out of you, darling?"

Their eyes locked in a moment of mutual understanding. Despite her parade of lovers over the years, it still openly tore her up to watch father and daughter exist hand in glove. She enjoyed cornering Wendy and pointing out all her flaws and shortcomings.

"Girl talk can get tiresome," she pressed.

Girl talk. Wait until Margo got a look at their new friend!

Ross smiled blandly. "I don't expect to be bored at all."

HER DAUGHTER'S BEDROOM.

One short week ago, Karen didn't even know she had a child. Now she was standing in her bedroom.

"This is really nice, Wendy!" she called out to compliment.

Wendy poked her head through her bathroom doorway, her small face puckered in doubt and hope. "You really mean it, Karen?"

"Of course I do!" she fervently assured her, forcing a smile. But Karen was aching inside. Wendy's sassy shell was onion-skin thin. She needed firm support.

Over and over again, she found herself about to explode with emotion. Karen wasn't accustomed to concealing her innermost feelings during personal moments. Of course, on-the-job experiences on the Las Vegas police force had taught her much about objectivity and self-control. But those were other people's crises, other people's children.

A personal relationship to Karen meant fervent commitment, infinite compassion, demonstrative affection with lots of touching and embracing.

Her fingers curled at her sides as she once again fought the urge to envelop Wendy in her arms and console her troubles away.

"Come out here and show me around," she coaxed. "You have a minute to spare for that."

Praise for the girl's nest proved to be a steadying tonic. Wendy emerged, dabbing her damp face with a towel. She beamed as she followed Karen's appraising eye. "We call this the loft room because it's at the very top of the house. Almost in the clouds, Daddy says."

The room was heavenly, Karen conceded. The ceiling followed the slanted roofline, and its rich walnut paneling matched the trim throughout the house. Polished oak furniture, obviously custom-made for the uniquely angled room was arranged in functional order. The decor was frilly tranquility, with puffy shades and bedspread in a minifloral print. It was all too perfect somehow, emanating an unused feel. Aside from a couple of small stuffed animals and a poster of a teenage heartthrob, the room could have belonged to any female of any age.

Karen casually wandered over to a bookshelf boasting some silver-framed photographs, looking for new insight into Wendy's life. They were all of Wendy and Ross. Skiing, cycling, mountain climbing. They were always smiling. That was the most important thing. They were happy together in each and every one.

"Cool, huh?" Wendy chirped behind her. "It's great having a super dad to do things with. He can do anything, Karen. He's big and strong and has power over everybody around here."

"You must really love him," Karen murmured, setting the last photo back in place.

"Well, sure I do!" she blurted back matter-of-factly.

"Do you ever play a game like say, oh, wondering what other kind of life you could've had?" Karen asked lightly. When Wendy wrinkled her nose in confusion, she added, "You know what I mean, honey, a wishing game, a game where you dream of the best life ever."

Wendy shrugged loosely. "Guess I don't know much about how other girls live, Karen. I wish my mom wouldn't come around and make us sad. But Daddy always makes everything better after," she reflected wistfully.

"Sounds like quite a man," Karen remarked on a forced high note.

"He's just right. And he'd do anything for me. Anything."

Karen nodded with a polite smile. "I am very glad to hear that." But despite Ross's devotion, this picture wasn't ideal, not by a long shot. Wendy was insecure and pampered. And she didn't seem to know how the rest of the world lived.

Ross Chandler would fall over dead if he ever had a glimpse into the past of Wendy's birth mother, streetwise Karen Bradford. Didn't he ever wonder about the child's roots? It was probably easy to forget about the adoption glitch. She certainly would in his place. Who wouldn't want to claim Wendy as his or her own even without the sharing of a common bloodline? She also suspected that Wendy had no idea that she was an adopted child. Given her frenzied reaction to Margo's arrival, Karen felt Wendy would've declared her distance in the most dramatic way. Detached herself by reminding Ross that Margo wasn't even her real mother, and she didn't have to see her if she didn't want to. But the girl had just fallen apart, hustling back here to please.

Adoption was still kept secret from some children, she supposed. But it wasn't the norm these days, was it? Deep inside her secret selfish psyche, Karen had come to hope that the girl already knew the truth. That she was fervently hoping to someday include her birth mother in her life.

Stew certainly knew her well, Karen deduced ruefully. She wasn't the observer type. She was the hands-on type. One look at Wendy and she wanted a stake in the girl's life. A stake she could not morally bring herself to claim.

The bottom line was clear. No matter what Wendy might know or not know, she was far too naive and fragile at this point to accept her lineage.

"I've got to find something to wear!" Wendy suddenly shrieked. She tore over to her large closet and pulled open the accordion doors. "And my hair!" With a cry of indecision, she rushed over to her dressing table and plunked down on the stool. "My brush, where's my brush?" She began to yank open drawers.

"I'll select an outfit from your closet while you fix your hair," Karen suggested, moving over to the rack jammed with neatly pressed clothing.

"*Kind!* You startled me!"

Karen whirled around at the sound of the German-sprinkled greeting. A plump woman with snow-white hair, dressed in a practical cotton print dress, was entering the room.

"Oh, Nanny Gee! Mother's here! I have to get ready!"

The old woman's round face sharpened. "Your *mutter hier?* What on earth could she want?"

"Don't matter!" the girl wailed, closing one drawer, opening another.

The nanny's attention shifted to the stranger at the closet. Karen promptly introduced herself in a capsuled greeting. "I'm Karen Ford, temporary tennis partner and singer in the Starlite Lounge."

"Ah, pleased to meet you," the woman rumbled, inspecting Karen without apology. "I am the family nanny." Karen was impressed with her. She was on the far side of sixty, but she had a strong, no-nonsense air about her—and all the obvious moves of a protective mother hen.

"Karen's helping me get ready, Nan," Wendy paused to explain to the disgruntled woman.

"No need to excite yourself so, *Kind*," she clucked in concern. "Not good for your stomach."

Wendy found her brush and straightened up for a look in the mirror. "My hair is nuked!"

Nanny Gee closed in on her charge with a confused tsk. "What does this 'nuked' mean?"

"Disaster!" Wendy translated.

"Nonsense!" the old woman scoffed gently with a soft pat to Wendy's head. "You are a sweet little girl with a lovely hairstyle."

"I wholeheartedly agree," Karen chimed in. She pulled an eyelet sundress off the rack. "How would this be?"

Wendy crinkled her nose. "The hem is wrinkled."

"Not very much," Karen objected. But Wendy was adamant so she replaced the hanger.

"Please find something else. Hurry. She doesn't like to wait. She—"

"Wendy! Darling!" A shrill, terse voice sang out from the doorway.

Just might show up unannounced. Karen inwardly finished Wendy's thought. Margo Chandler in person. By all appearances, the haughty, high-strung woman was everything Karen thought a mother shouldn't be.

# 6

"WENDY! DARLING!" Margo edgily repeated her gushy greeting. "I know you would've come looking for me, but mother's time is precious."

"Oh, yes, I . . ." Wendy balked at the chic peacock blue locomotive steaming her way across the plush cream carpet.

Karen was quick to note from her position at the closet that Ross was right behind her. Thank goodness!

He spared Karen a distressed, apologetic look that spoke of more family laundry out to dry.

But there was nowhere else on earth that she'd rather be. She'd actually made it inside this family for a close, intimate look.

Margo yanked the brush from Wendy's shaky hand and began to pull it through her daughter's long blond mane with vigorous tugs. "Such a mop! You really must get a cut, Wendy. A short, manageable style like mine is so popular right now. And especially perfect for the careless sort."

"Ouch!" Wendy squealed as the brush snagged some knotted hair.

"Damn it, Margo!" Ross immediately wedged himself between mother and daughter, firmly clamping onto Margo's arm as she raised the brush in the air for more momentum.

Margo stumbled off balance under his forceful tug, then noticed Karen for the first time. "Oh!"

Karen met Margo's gaze for a long, blazing moment. Stew had mentioned that Margo had been the one to personally pick up Baby Bradford at the hospital. Had she seen Karen in that narrow railed bed after the birth? Would she make the decade-old connection, place her as the spent sixteen-year-old girl in the Las Vegas maternity ward? Karen's appearance had certainly changed since that depressing low point. She'd been chunky right up to her chin, drained right down to her toes. And she'd worn the feathery hairstyle so popular back in the mid-eighties. Her heart pounded with apprehension as she faced her off and waited....

"Who the hell is she?" Margo blared. Her tone was meant to intimidate, but her obvious ignorance concerning Karen's identity overrode all else in the policewoman's mind.

"My friend," Wendy piped up in swift defense.

"Isn't she a little old?" Margo inquired meanly.

"Actually, Margo," Ross intervened with pleasure, "she is my protégée."

"Your what?" Margo demanded on a low, lethal tone.

Karen bit back a smile as Ross's expression grew wolfish.

"Wendy, why don't you go downstairs for a snack," he suggested with a significant look to the nanny. Nanny Gee quickly took her charge in hand and whisked her out the door.

"Since when have you been interested in taking on a protégée, Ross?"

"Since Tiffany left a gap in my entertainment lineup," he easily explained with an offhanded gesture. "Karen

t she'd gone completely haywire over all the dis-
pointments delivered and wanted satisfaction.

Karen the cop reacted to Margo as though she were
e wild-card wife in a nasty domestic dispute. With a
w swift moves, she had Margo neutralized, crowd-
g her against the closet door with her hands pinned
mly behind her back.

Margo's threats grew more colorful as Ross stepped
close, observing the scene with the same blend of
isbelief and curiosity one might have in a traffic ac-
ident.

"I'm not hurting her, Ross," Karen assured him, eas-
y controlling the writhing woman.

Ross's expression hardened in shame. "You'd have
een well within your rights to attack in self-defense."

"That's a fine thing!" Margo sputtered in outrage.

Ross moved closer. "Now are you going to play
ice?"

"She's humiliating me, you bastard!"

"You humiliated yourself by lunging at her," Ross
larified. "This is a self-defense hold. She could've let
ou get in the first claw and clawed you right back."

"Tell her to release me!" she stormed at him.

"In due time."

"Now!"

"I tried this the pleasant way, and you just weren't
tting the message."

"I'll scream," she threatened.

"And summon Wendy? I'm sure you agree that she
ouldn't see this."

She shook her dark head. "Don't—don't want her to
how wicked you are!"

Ross ignored her attempt to divert the blame. He'd
n trying for the longest time to reach her on Wen-

Ford's singing in her place. She's a gifted amateur on her
way to the top."

"Isn't she a little young?"

He clucked mockingly. "I thought you said she was
a little too old."

"You follow my meaning," she said nastily.

"But you do not follow mine," he retorted. "Karen is
exactly what she seems, a young singer learning the
ropes. A charming lady who both Wendy and I respect."

Margo sidled up to him. "I like them young myself,"
she begrudgingly admitted in a whisper. "But to call her
your protégée . . ."

Ross knew damn well that Margo had cruder terms
to describe her more youthful, vulnerable male friends.
Words that reflected their impermanent, meaningless
status.

He shook his head, running his hands through his
hair. "I'm telling you the simple truth here, and you re-
fuse to believe it."

Karen folded her arms across her chest, returning his
helpless look with a wry one. They both knew damn
well that Margo had tagged her as a protégée of another sort. But Karen didn't mind. If she could be in-
strumental in repelling this viper for Wendy's sake, so
much the better.

"Now I'm beginning to better understand why you're
cutting out the extras, trying to shuffle me off to Boston," Margo ranted knowingly.

"I truly want you to get a grip on your life," he insisted. "Make a fresh start, the way I finally intend to
do."

"But after all these years, our arrangement has—"

"Has become old and stagnant," he finished with sharp impatience.

"What will people say?"

"People with any sense will say that we're finally moving forward," he reasoned.

"Precious protégée, eh?" Margo's glare burned holes through the exercise-ruffled blonde, made up with only a trace of coral lipstick, patiently keeping a quiet distance. Doubt spread over Margo's artistically drawn features as she did some calculating. "She hasn't been around here long. I'd have heard about her. And if she's filling in for Tiffany, she'll soon be out of a job, as well." Drawing a feline smile, she turned to speak to Karen. "My scruples force me to caution you about our fickle Ross, Miss Ford."

"Scruples?" Ross choked. Under his slack-jawed expression, Margo advanced on her rival.

Karen straightened, her spine stiff and her temper simmering. "I really don't think any warning is necessary, Mrs. Chandler."

"Oh, but we're so unevenly matched," Margo insisted on a shrill note.

"Not at all. Really." Karen smiled thinly. "I am in total command of my life and have been so for quite some time."

"There are a lot of little rituals that go on in our circles that a child like you would have no way of comprehending."

"Margo . . ." Ross's growl was an equal mix of warning and trepidation. He hadn't banked on this territorial confrontation. He had figured her far too arrogant and vain to fight for him. Ross ran a hand through his short dark hair. He was surrounded by women at his resort, but he would never attain the wisdom to un-

derstand them, much less second-gue
tossed this hellcat at his innocent employ
was going to have to call her off.

"You see," Margo continued in a conspi
"he enjoys an ornament on his arm and a
in his bed. And quite frankly, dear, so do
a prerequisite to the altar, no matter wh
promises he's made. For though we can n
together, we just can't seem to live without
It's left us in sort of a marital limbo."

"Margo!" Ross roared. "Shut up!"

Margo blinked prettily in feigned innoce
ing in the space between the pair. "Oh, don't
let something out of the bag!"

"The mistake was letting you out of yo
Karen retorted snidely.

Ross shared Margo's surprise over the rem
Karen was churning with a private torment ne
of them could even begin to understand. Ha
interviewed this woman at all before tur
Wendy? It was so unlike the practical schoo
make such a damaging mistake. Perhaps sh
spoken to Ross. Perhaps he'd handled th
arrangements and then sent his wife to
pickup.

Either way, it was a horrible lapse in judg
aunt's part and added further substance t
lief that Wendy never should have left he
first place.

The next few moments were a fast-pace
advanced on her, primed for attack wi
and fingernails arched. By the threats a
spewing from her lovely-shaped mout

dy's behalf. Somehow illustrate how the girl felt in her hands. "Just think for a moment about how you feel this very minute, locked in a helpless, powerless position," he directed tersely. "This is how uncomfortable you make your own little girl feel each and every time you come near her."

"No!"

"Yes," he insisted. "I am sick and tired of waiting for you to see the light, Margo."

"We're two of a kind," she protested with a knowing glitter in her eyes.

"Not anymore," he vehemently denied. "The selfish, egotistical man you married no longer exists. Our little girl has whipped me into a gushy, softhearted chump."

Her lovely mouth took on an ugly sneer. "I don't believe it."

His jaw compressed. "Believe it. And believe that we are finally through. We share nothing but the same last name."

"Wendy is still—"

"She will no longer be your pipeline to me and my wallet!" he cut in harshly. "I'm tired of assuring her that you mean well. I'm a lousy actor, and she's just not buying it anymore. I know you have a legal right to visit, but I want you to freely give it up. If you don't, I'll haul your butt back into court and make a public spectacle out of you. What will your precious people think of that?"

Margo made an effort to squirm away from Karen's grip. "You wouldn't!"

"I would do anything for Wendy," he warned on a menacing note. "And you clearly recognize my tone. Though I've never used it on you before..."

Margo's eyes flickered in comprehension and apprehension. "All right! Just make her let me go!"

"Agree to my terms?"

"Yes!"

Ross laid a gentle hand on Karen's shoulder. "I believe that Margo would like to leave us."

Karen loosened her hold and Margo teetered out of reach, righting herself on her high heels. "I won't have to do anything to get you back, Ross!" she announced in a last-ditch attempt to recapture her dignity. "I happen to believe that no matter what our legal ties are, we are a pair." With a quick look in Wendy's full-length mirror, she breezed out the door.

"SHE TRULY IS DEMENTED, isn't she?"

Karen made the diagnosis of Margo a short time later as they sat together in the living room on his butter-soft leather sofa.

Ross nodded with a deep, rueful sigh. "Yes, she's apparently taken a further slide into her own neurotic world. You can be sure, however," he added rather awkwardly, "that she doesn't have any sort of infinite power over me."

"Oh, Ross." Karen gave the hand on his knee a squeeze. "I didn't believe her claim. Besides, your love life certainly isn't any of my business."

But he wanted it to be. With every passing hour, Ross wanted Karen all the more. Wanted her to be his love life. She was the prototype of his dream partner. Fair-haired, intelligent, compassionate and exciting. Pretty without perfection. Charming without plastic coyness. Seemingly unaffected by show-business glitter.

A jolt of fear coursed through him. After all his years of floating from one relationship to another with no direction, was he even capable of spotting the real thing when he saw it?

He was! He owed himself that much faith. And he owed Wendy the chance at a more proper female role model.

Karen was watching him in cautious expectation. "Is there something wrong?"

"Only the obvious," he quietly replied, staring pensively into the dark stone fireplace before them. "But you've done everything right."

His positive attitude gave Karen the courage to explore the baffling situation further. How could this man have ended up with that woman? How could that woman ever have wanted her child in the first place? "Margo seems like an impossible personality. Was she always this way?"

"Well, I guess there was a time when I was a bit impossible myself," he confessed, flashing her a smile. "To be honest, there were several years, earlier on in our marriage, when she had every right to believe that she had me hooked." He stared into her brilliant blue eyes for traces of surprise or judgment. He read nothing but simple curiosity. Encouraged, he continued. "We married fifteen years ago at the age of twenty. I was full of myself back then. Driven, ambitious, backed by my father's money. He was a renowned jeweler who, along with my mother, lived the high life. He introduced my older brother, Ron, and me to the finer things of life from the start, as well. When we finished college, he literally handed over a part of his wealth, encouraged us to multiply it in our own interests. Ron and I did just that. We rounded up some investors, opened this resort and built it up to its present size."

A flash of pride brightened his expression. "It was just a shabby little operation when we bought it. Had a few log cabins near the natural lake out back." He gestured toward the open kitchen and the window beyond. "After a few years, we expanded with the Cannes connection. That casino is smaller but just as popular as this one."

"Started at the top," Karen noted. "Lucky break."

"Yes," he admitted without apology. "But there were things lacking in our family. My parents loved us in their own way, but it was Grethal who raised us, nurtured us. Which brings me to Margo," he said on a note of regret. "To a selfish, ambitious young man like I was, she seemed like the perfect addition to the master plan. Calculating, cultured, intelligent. Margo is one of the Boston Paynes. That was a favorable social connection in my family's eyes.

"And there were good times in the beginning. Too good. We really enjoyed ourselves on the global party circuit. A self-absorbed couple with big dreams. But eventually it wasn't enough. I wanted children. Margo wasn't so sure. But she did eventually indulge me. Unfortunately, Wendy's arrival marked the beginning of Margo's deterioration. I grew up, eagerly accepting the responsibilities of parenthood. Margo bent the other way, sort of disintegrating with the strain. She immediately discovered that she didn't want to share me with anyone. Not even Wendy."

"That's awful!" Karen couldn't help blurting out.

"I know," he affirmed quietly. "Thank heavens for Nanny Grethal. After the love and support she gave Ron and me, it seemed only natural that she play an important role in Wendy's upbringing, too. It was the wisest move I've ever made. As you can imagine, my business obligations are enormous and time-consuming. When Margo's inadequacies became sadly apparent, Nanny Gee was already here, prepared to step in as the loving grandma."

"So you finally reached your limit with her," Karen prodded. "Filed for the divorce?"

"Yes," he soberly reported. "She developed a gambling problem on top of her frustrations and jealousies—or perhaps because of them. The compulsion was manageable at first, an in-house problem taken care of by my staff. But she soon tired of her controlled environment and went on the prowl down in Las Vegas. Lost some sizable amounts of cash. I cleaned up the messes at first, but it soon became intolerable."

Despite his open misery, Karen couldn't help but think of the most vulnerable victim. "Poor Wendy, bearing the brunt of the mistake, too."

Sadness and remorse deepened in his arresting features. "Yes. I've been running in circles far too long. Humoring Margo out of an inflated sense of responsibility, hoping that she could somehow give Wendy the approval she so craves. But I am more determined than ever to shut Margo out completely. I've suspected for a while that she was really crumbling, but I had no idea just how bad she was, until she came at you." He flashed her an apologetic smile. "Thanks for understanding. For not tossing her out the window."

"She's a damaged personality who needs help," Karen remarked.

He nodded vigorously. "I've tried numerous times to get her some. I've appealed to her family, as well. But the Payne clan doesn't want her unless she comes home willingly. And that Margo must do on her own."

"Yes." She knew much about treatment, but couldn't let on without hinting at her real occupation. She'd already risked his suspicion by subduing Margo. "I think I surprised her with my strength."

"Me, too," he confessed with a sheepish look. "Had I known how handy you are, I probably wouldn't have risked your ire the way I did."

"As your protégée?" she lilted, humor touching her brilliant blue eyes.

A grin split his face. "Yeah."

"That was pretty sneaky."

"I told her the simple truth. She chose not to believe it."

"To no surprise, I'm sure," she averred. "But I understand that you were trying to shoo her away from Wendy."

He nodded, his fingers skimming the soft curve of her cheek. "Mostly. But it was a whole lot of fun, you know, pretending just for a little while that you were my eager pupil. . . ."

Karen smiled wistfully. He was a little too late. About ten years and one child too late. But his magnetism was disarmingly sexy and appealing. And he was preparing to kiss her.

And she wanted him to do it. As foolishly risky and complicated as this flirtation was, she found him irresistible. He was shifting on the sofa now, closing in over her with strong, lean limbs. She welcomed his advances, parting her lips in sultry encouragement. He closed his mouth over hers with a heady moan of pleasure. She inhaled, absorbing his own delicious scent spiced with after-shave. Her fingers moved to his shoulders, first skimming, then digging, as his hands and tongue explored her intimately.

"Mmm . . ." He pried his lips from hers, kissing her temples. "Maybe we could do that thing."

Karen fluttered her tawny lashes in confusion. "What thing?"

"You know," he crooned, "the hold. Does it work on the bed?"

She gasped. "What?"

He chuckled then, his eyes crinkling with boyish humor.

"Hey, I want you to know that I don't tumble for just anybody," she said, flirting under his teasing gaze.

"I don't either," he confessed softly. "I just wanted to stir you up a little."

"Why?"

He fingered some of her soft golden hair. "Because you seem so unflappable. I've felt a challenge from the start to upset you, much in the same way that you upset me."

"I didn't mean to—"

He pressed his fingers to her lips. "I'm not complaining. You bring out the randy teenager in me. Make me want to play a little for a change. I simply want you to join in."

"I do like you, Ross. A lot."

He was openly pleased. "I've shut myself off from new beginnings for far too long. But there's something about you. A feeling, a chemistry, that has given me a new kind of hope. Does that sound crazy?"

"I'd say we're acting crazy together," she murmured, tracing her nail along the cleft in his chin. "When I planned this temporary getaway, I never dreamed that you and I—" She broke off, at a loss for a brief moment. "Well, I simply wasn't expecting this. . . ."

He lifted a rueful brow. "Margo was right about you being young, Karen. It's not my intention to take advantage of you in any way."

"I've done my share of living, Ross," she hastened to convince him.

"I thought so," he admitted.

Her heart jumped a little. "Why?"

He lifted a shoulder. "It's usually mirrored in the eyes."

Karen took a steadying breath. He was bound to want details about her personal life. It was a sign that he was a caring man.

"A young woman fresh to the game usually holds the starry-eyed look worn by my own daughter," he went on to expound. "Your eyes twinkle with a captivating blend of wisdom and tenderness. You have a story already."

"There really isn't much to tell," she claimed evasively.

"I don't believe you. But I do love a mystery, so I'll just search for clues. Deep, exciting clues . . ." Hooking her chin in the crook of his finger, he guided her mouth back to his.

Karen gave in to the pleasures of his kiss, feeling dizzy and exhilarated and frightened in one dynamite surge.

"Hey, what are you guys doing?"

The pair broke contact at the sound of Wendy's indignant approach.

"Kissing," Ross replied succinctly. "You have a problem with that?"

"Guess not," she chirped after some deliberation, bouncing down between them on the sofa. "As long as you don't take up all her time. She's my friend."

Ross sighed, winding an arm around his daughter's slender shoulders. "I had a talk with your mother. I'm afraid she's feeling a bit sicker than usual."

"She hurt me with that brush," Wendy confided with a wince. "She's never done that before. Only yelled."

Karen couldn't help but reach out and stroke the girl's lush mane of hair.

"I want to love her, but I can't!" Wendy lamented with a pleading look to Karen. "She's always mean. I never do anything right. I'll bet you had a real nice mom, didn't you, Karen?"

Karen slid her fingers through Wendy's hair, deliberating over how much of her own past she should reveal. But perhaps it would help the child to know that her situation wasn't unique. She was already so isolated and set apart from the outside world. "No, Wendy," Karen softly intimated. "My mother has some emotional problems. She eventually didn't want to deal with me at all. I moved in with a relative."

"Where was your dad?" Wendy piped up, patting Ross's knee.

"He died quite a long time ago," Karen said simply, her lower lip trembling behind her smile.

How shortsighted of her to think she could come and collect information without revealing any! It still pained her deeply whenever she recalled her yesterdays. But this was the price she apparently was to pay for crashing into her daughter's life.

Who knew better than she that every move one made had a price tag attached?

"I think it would be best if you had no contact with Margo for the time being," Ross was now offering his daughter in consolation.

"But how can you stop her, Dad? And my birthday's next weekend, too! She loves parties where she can get attention. I don't want the girls to laugh at her—at me. It's already so hard to make friends at school. They just don't seem to like me much. I hoped this party would help. But if she comes, it'll be totally wrecked."

Karen bit her lip as Ross went on with a list of guarantees. Margo would not be crashing her little party. Margo would not be railing at her anymore. But his assurances that she was indeed a winner all of the time, that nobody was better, seemed a bit overdone.

Karen listened with a measure of sympathy and exasperation. Ross's intentions with the girl were consistently the best. But in an effort to compensate for Margo, he was just too doting. Imagine, encouraging the employees to rig losses on the tennis courts. Reiterating in different ways that Wendy was superior to everyone in sight. No wonder she had trouble socializing in school!

Wendy didn't need such inflated, unrealistic boosts. She needed guidance, a firmer kind of love. She needed some survival training to prepare her for the real world.

Karen felt a renewing surge of power and purpose. It was fate that had sent her here. Her baby needed her. Really truly needed her. Happy birthday, baby. Your real mother is here to help set it right.

# 7

THE DECISION TO LEAVE the chalet shortly thereafter was a tough one for Karen. She was tired, however, and sensed that Ross and Wendy could use a little privacy. It had been an incredibly exhausting day. And she still had her show tonight!

Despite it all, she'd had the overwhelming urge to stay on, enjoy the light supper that Nanny Gee had offered her. Karen had sensed an unexpected alliance with the family's surrogate grandmother. The old nanny reminded Karen of her aunt in numerous ways, with her bustling demeanor, the no-nonsense attitude.

Seasoned spinsters and proud of it.

Both hardworking women of the old school, who shared an amazing number of characteristics. Karen couldn't help but compare them and draw wisdom from the analogy. Finding a prototype of Irene, along with the passage of time, was bound to help Karen put her own upbringing in better perspective.

Irene's limitations as a parent were becoming easier to accept and forgive. Stew had been absolutely right not to spare her any of the details on Irene's philosophy and decisions.

It was only through learning the truth that a person could come to a clear, unconditional understanding of her world.

Veracity was putting Karen's life in balance, bringing her the peace she so wanted for herself.

But what of Wendy's life? What sort of action would serve her best?

Truth was basically a good thing. It was the timing and the delivery that made revelations sticky. Karen prided herself on building wisdom and good judgment over the years. She should be more than capable of making the right choices, if and when they arose.

This just might be one of those cases where the truth would never surface.

The idea of letting go of her daughter at the end of the week was becoming a wrenching one. Would righting a few of the wrongs in Wendy's life be enough to sustain Karen?

She shook her head to chase away the realities. She couldn't bear to forecast their last day together. Not yet.

Not when she and Ross were on the brink of their first night. Their first real night together. She had the deep-rooted feeling that he was going to make his move after her show....

She was still mulling over all the steamy possibilities, in a hot bubbly tub when the telephone rang on the tiled wall. She sat up, reached out an eager, sudsy hand and drew the receiver down to her ear.

"Hi, honey."

"Ross."

His name was a husky caress on her tongue as she sank back into the water.

"Did I catch you at an awkward moment?"

She shifted position with a splash.

His knowing chuckle filled the wire, causing Karen's senses to stir with longing, as though he were right there in the bathroom with her, enjoying the intimate moment.

Maybe he would want to pop over right now....

Should she let him?

"Did you want something, Ross?" she mustered the courage to ask.

"Yes." There was a heavy sigh on the line. One of hesitation and apology. "I wanted to thank you again for helping today."

"It was my pleasure, truly. How is Wendy?"

"Fine. She gets pretty spunky after these scenes with Margo, so it's tough to say. If it's going to affect her, it'll be tonight, in the form of a nightmare."

"Oh." Karen swallowed hard, discovering there was a lump in her throat. She knew what was coming.

"I think it would be best if I stuck close to home through the evening. It's hard for Grethal to rouse herself to comfort Wendy in the throes of one of her midnight horror shows. Wendy has to be thoroughly awakened, assured that everything is all right."

"Tell her I wish her the sweetest of dreams," Karen murmured.

"Thank you so much."

The pathetic gratitude in his tone made up for the letdown of his call. If he'd been dating women who didn't understand such things, he'd undoubtedly been dating the wrong kind of woman.

"Well, Ross, the show will go on—" she said in closing.

"No! Wait. Karen, are you still there?"

She laughed in reply. "Still planted in place."

"I want to set up something for tomorrow morning."

"Oh?"

"Wendy and I usually start off our Sunday with a round of golf and some brunch in the hotel dining room. Care to join us?"

"Yes! I'd love that!" Karen closed her eyes with a wince. She sounded desperate. But amazingly, his responding sigh of relief was just as unambiguous.

"Great. Meet you in the hotel lobby tomorrow around eight."

The corollaries of her acceptance sent her shooting out of the tub. She hung up the phone, whirled on the blue oval rug, then bent over to unplug the drain. She was in a tizzy. Right where she belonged! She didn't have a thing to wear on the golf course. Which was no wonder, because she'd never played golf! She grabbed a fluffy white towel from the rod and began to dry off. She'd have to make a quick run down to the resort pro shop for an outfit and maybe a quick lesson.

After the tromping she'd given Wendy on the tennis courts this was bound to be a turning of the tables.

"HEY, KAREN, ARE YOU even trying?"

Wendy stood just outside the rim of the plush course's second green the following morning, her gloved hands planted on her hips. She looked utterly professional in her lavender short set—and utterly aggravated.

Karen gripped her putter tightly, resting her weight on it for a moment. "Yes!" she called back with a limp wave. "I'm trying!"

Ross strolled up to Karen on the green and stroked her arm. "Relax," he softly coaxed.

Karen bobbed her head. "Yeah. Yeah, I know that." She looked down at the offensive little golf ball at her feet. Six times she'd tried to sink it into the tiny hole. Six times it rolled right past it. If she could just give it the right tap with this awkward little club. She'd managed to sink it on the first one, but it had just been luck.

Ross smothered a laugh behind a cough as he watched her test her swing. She was so politically correct, outfitted in a powder blue knit sunsuit and matching cap straight out of his pro shop, mumbling pat instructions routinely provided by the resort's pro. But still, she was so obviously out of place. The rookie all over again. Telling her that she was green on the green was almost too irresistible. But he just couldn't do it. She was already on the verge of bending her clubs over something. Or someone.

Karen stiffened when Ross moved behind her to give her shoulders a squeeze.

"I can't hide it anymore," he whispered close to her ear. "I know everything."

If she wasn't so frustrated, his words might have frightened her. As it was, his claim sounded way too cocky, a boast about knowing all the secrets in the universe, rather than just her small personal confidences.

She straightened up, twisting to meet his gaze. "What *everything* is making you so damn insufferable?"

"That this is your first time on the links, of course."

"This is so embarrassing," she broke down and confessed.

"It's charming," he disagreed. "You wanted to come, so you took steps to fit in. I'm flattered."

"Oh..." Karen could feel a blush dashing her cheeks.

"You aren't that bad, really," he consoled. "It's just that I recognize my own merchandise, and the pro mentioned your abrupt visit."

Wendy stalked over, casting a shadow on Karen's ball. "Are you letting me take the lead?" she demanded tersely. "Because if you are, I'm really gonna be mad at you!"

"But you like to win," Ross reminded her.

"But it feels good to be winning on my own for once," Wendy protested anxiously. "If that's what I'm doing."

"That is exactly what you're doing," Karen heartily assured her.

"I don't believe it," Wendy insisted, giving her shorts and cap a straightening tug. "Nobody can get a score as crummy as yours!"

"Remember how kind and patient Karen was with your tennis game?" Ross interjected mildly.

"Yes, Dad! But—"

"Karen is new to the game," he explained, signaling the foursome behind them to putt. "It's only fair that we pull her out of this mess."

"Oh!" New understanding lighted up Wendy's face.

New understanding . . . and a measure of pity, Karen noted, wrinkling her nose in discontent.

"I'll show her, Dad."

"No, I'll do it," he swiftly cut in, pressing his fingers deeper into Karen's shoulders in a possessive move. "You aren't . . . tall enough."

Once the foursome was on their way off the green, Ross slid his hands down her arms with encouraging noises. "That's right, keep hands in a parallel position, thumbs off the center line of the grip. Bend your knees. Good. Now, test your stance by rotating your hips and shoulders."

A shiver coursed along her spine as she pressed her body back into his. The directions were on the level— the exact ones the pro had given her yesterday. But Ross's snug position behind her was so obviously contrived. And so obviously delicious.

"What are you doing, Ross?" she gasped, her eye on Wendy as she moved toward the golf cart holding her bag of clubs.

"Checking your body position, of course," he crooned in her ear.

"The pro approached the sport differently," she saucily rejoined.

"Maybe the pro was approaching a whole different sport," he returned smoothly. Before she could respond to the innuendo, Ross's hands were over hers, and their bodies were swinging slightly. He took control of the club and tapped the ball into the hole. "Ah, see. A hole in twelve."

"A hole in seven," she corrected brightly. "Shall we move on?"

They played half of the eighteen-hole course, then strolled back to the clubhouse pulling their carts behind them.

"So how does it feel, Wendy," Karen asked good-naturedly. "Showing up this old lady?"

"You're not old," Wendy objected. "Especially compared to Dad."

"Thanks a lot," Ross grumbled, tugging at the bill of her cap.

"It does feel real good," Wendy confided with a giggle. "I'm gonna ask everybody to try their best at some of these games from now on. See if I can really beat them."

"That's great," Karen said with maternal pride. She was making a difference. Even by losing, she was winning!

"So what do you say, shall I treat you girls to a meal?" Ross suggested as they returned their clubs to an attendant outside the clubhouse.

"Sunday brunch, Dad?" Wendy challenged. "It's complimentary to the guests."

"I'm trying to look like a big shot," he uttered secretively, tipping his head toward a skeptical Karen.

Wendy snapped her gum, rolling her eyes. "Sure, Dad, sure."

The laughing threesome piled into an awning-covered cart and drove back to the hotel. An employee stopped Ross in the lobby outside the restaurant, so Karen took Wendy inside herself.

Ross soon caught up with the pair in the spacious Southwestern-style room of glass and stone, only to find them in line with the guests! Quelling his exasperation, he moved up behind them to grasp each by an elbow.

"This isn't necessary," he chided. "All you had to do was tell the maître d' or anybody on staff that you were here." To his surprise, Wendy instantly deferred to Karen, staring up at her with starry eyes.

Karen forced herself to meet his agitated gaze with sparkling levity. She was sure they'd peel the grapes if so ordered! But with Ross out of the way for a moment, she couldn't resist another opportunity to put a dent of reality into Wendy's magical world.

"I thought it might be fun for Wendy to wait in line for a change," she announced brightly.

His brows drew together. "My staff will think I'm nuts."

"Oh, waiting builds character," she couldn't help but scoff.

"Maybe I'm not accustomed to waiting for anything," he returned silkily.

"There are rewards for taking your time," she insisted, gesturing to the vast variety of steaming steel pans of meats and potatoes and huge bowls of cold salads. "Gives you a chance to pick out exactly what you want."

"I already know exactly what I want," he assured her with a look hot enough to melt the stiffest, golf-weary joints. He wanted his way. All the way.

"Well, I sure don't!" Wendy spouted off, eagerly grabbing a plate. "There's some food up here on the buffet that I've never even seen before. You've been hiding this fun line thing from me for too long, Dad."

Ross rolled his eyes with incredulous surrender. "Oh, dear daughter, I hope you can find it in your heart to forgive me."

"Oh, sure," she called over her shoulder as she scooped food onto her plate.

Karen heard a cluck in the shell of her ear. "Miss Ford, do you have any idea what kinds of ruckus you're causing?"

Turning to Ross and blinking prettily, she deliberately mistook the meaning of his words. "You're causing the ruckus. By holding up this line!"

# 8

KAREN JOINED her backup band in the Starlite Lounge for some rehearsal later on that afternoon. The four-piece combo was already on stage when she arrived, hunched around the baby grand piano, going over a new piece. Dinah Delray was with them, dressed in matching yellow shorts and top that set off her red hair in a very appealing way. The leggy ex-showgirl was the first to spot Karen weaving her way through the setup crew down on the floor.

"I was afraid you forgot!" Dinah called out with a cheery wave.

"Just sidetracked," Karen called back, climbing the bank of stairs near the dark velvet curtains. She was greeted with a round of good-humored murmurs about playing up to the boss.

Karen advanced on Dinah and the young male musicians with a jutting chin and a sparkle in her blue eyes. "Okay, you guys. Just for the record, I am not an opportunist hoping to edge into a permanent pos—job," she corrected, hoping to play down the obvious implication.

"Tiffany would terminate you if you tried," Mel, the bearded sax player cracked, causing another round of chuckles.

"We're just giving you the customary initiation treatment," added the lanky blond, Curt, tapping her shoulder with one of his drumsticks. "You were too damn nervous last night to take the heat. So we postponed your dues until today."

Willy, their talented, long-haired pianist, gave Karen a thoughtful perusal from her tumbling blond hair down to her lime green blouse and tight blue jeans. "You've got two separate faces," he crooned in fascination.

Karen's heart raced at the surprising remark. "What, Willy?"

"I mean, dressed for the stage, you're a rangy cat. Dangerous. And now, in the daylight, you're a cuddly kitten. Sweet."

"Tiffany's different," Mel explained. "She's the same sort of babe around the clock. Probably sleeps in her makeup."

"A little lipstick and blush gets me through the day," Karen admitted.

"Gawd, you're young," Dinah complained with a snap of her gum.

"Of course, this room takes on a whole new face at night, too," she observed in an effort to shift the subject from her. She made a sweeping gesture across the domed theater. "Dim the lights, toss in some mood music and some wine, and you're on another plane of existence."

"You're all right, Ford," Willy complimented her with a wink.

"Initiation over then?" she gibed, with a hand on her hip.

"Sure," Dinah assured her. "You got your stars for beating Wendy in tennis."

"She really is a sweet little girl," Karen rushed on in her defense.

"We agree," Mel hastily placated. "But we all gotta learn to lose once in a while."

"This resort is like a small town, with its secrets and gossip," Curt explained. "Believe me, we know what the kid is up against with Margo. And we're all playing at her party, as our gift."

Karen brimmed with pleasure. "I've offered to sing. And help her with anything else."

"Ross will be grateful," Mel teased, moving toward his saxophone case.

Karen flashed him a thin, tolerant smile as she moved around the piano for a look at the sheet music. His reaction was natural. It did appear that she was merely buttering Ross up by befriending his daughter. It probably happened all the time. Let them think what they wanted. It only added to her cover.

Of course, one thing that wasn't contrived was the sexual tension growing between her and the resort owner. He was going to seduce her and she wanted him to!

"Oh, by the way," Dinah said, breaking into her thoughts, "Justine called a little while ago."

Karen's rounded jaw sagged. "What did she have to say?"

"Not much. Just wondered how you were getting along."

"What did you tell her, Dinah?"

Dinah's generous mouth curved. "Only the wonderful truth. That you are a hit with everyone right up to the boss himself."

Karen had intended to call Stew's law office tomorrow during working hours with a vague update. But Dinah's report took care of that little job. Justine was no doubt pleased to hear that her plan to edge Karen into the inner circle of the Pleasure Palace was so successful. Let her pass it on to Stew. Perfect.

"Oh, and of course I told her how dear you've been to Wendy," Dinah went on to add. "How remarkably involved you've become in the girl's welfare."

Karen's smile and spine stiffened in alert. Not so perfect.

"And I mentioned how Ross is utterly captivated by you because of your natural charms and the qualities you share with Wendy."

"She wants me to call her back as soon as possible, I imagine," Karen predicted with a tap to her pressed lips.

"Why, yes, she does! The sooner the better, she said." Dinah gave her a pat on the back. "You are popular, aren't you?"

"Oh, my, yes!" Karen agreed brightly.

Stew was going to kill her. Justine would hold her down and Stew would do the strangling. But she didn't care. Never in her whole life had anything ever felt so right. She didn't know if or how she was going to reveal herself to Ross. But she was already aching to tell him. Ready to step in as Wendy's birth mother and accept the caregiving responsibilities.

Was Ross ready to hear the good news she had to offer? Surely, with the passage of time and Margo's increasing problems, Ross had wondered whatever had happened to the young girl who had given birth to his beloved daughter. But he'd so overly protected Wendy from all the normal bumps and bruises in everyday living, that it was impossible to predict how he would react to the news.

Furthermore, he would have to confess to the girl that he wasn't her natural father. It was possible that he couldn't bring himself to give up that position.

Did she have a right to ask him to do it?

Time and patience were the answer. She would allow their relationship to deepen and hope that fate would open the right doors.

AFTER THEIR SEXY VERBAL exchanges during the day, Karen fully expected to find Ross waiting in her dressing room that night after the eleven o'clock show. Instead she found a long white box in his place on the love seat.

Was this a message? An invitation?

She flew across the room in her metallic dress and matching silver heels to peel off the cover. Nestled in green tissue paper, she found a dozen long-stemmed roses and a small white envelope. She sank onto the cushions to read his message with the eagerness of a girl on prom night.

Of course, she'd missed the prom at seventeen. After the pregnancy, she'd completed her high school education at home with Irene, graduating several months after her class.

Feeling way beyond her years by then, she'd buffered the social disappointments with the consoling truth that she had nothing in common with the boys her age. But deep in her heart, she, too, had wanted to play dress up, look in the mirror and see a flushed beauty and eyes full of wonder.

She fingered the envelope with a whimsical smile.

The dream of romance and glamour was still alive somewhere deep in her heart and was coming to life a decade later through Ross and this job.

Despite reminding herself that this situation was temporary and based on illusion, she couldn't help immersing herself in it.

After a long, pensive moment, she opened the envelope and extracted the small white note inside.

> Business has kept me away.
> Sorry, Ross.

"So you shall not dance at the ball, after all, m'dear." With a heaving sigh of disappointment, she tossed the note into the box and replaced the cover. She rose from the love seat, inadvertently catching another glimpse of herself in one of the room's many mirrors. She drew back, startled by her own face! Then she tentatively leaned closer, pushing back her tide of blond hair, anxiously surveying her expression. The face staring back at her beneath her striking stage makeup was desolate.

She had it bad for him. Worse than she thought. It was all happening so quickly, as though they'd been forced onto a roller-coaster ride together without the usual sort of dating foundation. But how to get close to a man you were keeping so many secrets from . . .

It was an unbelievable, romantic windfall.

A foolish game for a sensible woman to play. Karen had worked so hard her whole life through to reach her level of achievement. Nothing had ever come easy. Not once.

So what about this man and her daughter? Was finding them a reward for all the struggling, the good intentions, the bad breaks?

Dear lord, she hoped so!

And he'd cared enough to send the flowers.

Had the sense to know she'd expect him. Be disappointed.

It seemed he was right in stride with her on this magical journey.

A sharp knock interrupted her musings. Let it be him. Please. Karen grasped the knob and pulled the door open, her face beaming. In a fraction of a second, she took in the white knit shirt worn by many of the men in Ross's employ, then the smiling face of Walt, her assigned escort.

"Ready to return to the hotel, Karen?" he inquired.

"Ah, yes, Walt," she replied with forced cheeriness. "Just let me slip into my Reeboks."

Several minutes later, Karen emerged from the back entrance with a shimmery black shawl draped over her silver dress, white leather shoes on her feet. The burly Walt was at her side, with the box of roses tucked under his arm like a football.

Karen paused as the fine hairs on the back of her neck came to attention. When she was out on the streets on the job, the signal meant only one thing.

She was being watched.

A quick, darting look around confirmed her suspicions. Ross was standing five feet away, leaning against the trunk of an old cedar, his hands in the pockets of his black gabardine slacks, the sleeves of his white shirt rolled up over his solid tan forearms. His stance was relaxed, but she could feel his tension. It crackled in the space between them like static electricity.

"Hi," she said breathlessly, clutching the handle of her tote a little tighter.

"Hi." He emerged into the moonlight from the shadows with easy grace, the same elegant panther of the first night.

But he was more suitor than boss this time.

The possessive gleam in his dark brown eyes was unmistakable as he touched her shoulder.

"I'll take her back, Walt. Thanks."

"Sure, Ross." The escort shoved the box under Ross's free arm and swiftly disappeared back inside the nightclub.

"Thought you were busy with business," Karen commented lightly.

"I hurried."

Her stomach fluttered. "Oh, yeah?"

"Yeah."

She swallowed hard as his fingers curled around her bare arm. "The flowers are lovely."

"I arranged for them hours ago. When I was certain I'd never make it."

"But you did make it."

"Would you rather walk or ride, songbird?"

"Walk, I think. The act takes a lot out of me, but I prefer to wind down on the move. Makes it easier to sleep."

"But what about your heels?"

Karen lifted the full swingy hem of her dress to expose her leather athletic shoes.

He chuckled low in his throat. "You are full of surprises."

"Guilty."

They started down the sidewalk sloping away from the lounge. There were bursts of laughter and music in the warm, breezy night air. Colored lights and carnival magic surrounded them.

"I suppose Wendy was worn out?" Karen ventured, struggling to temper her interest. "It's been quite a weekend."

"I stopped by the house around nine to tuck her in and she was still wide awake, full of talk about you and her birthday. Tired and energized at the same time. But I don't expect any bad dreams to surface tonight."

"So Margo didn't do any lingering damage," Karen concluded hopefully.

"It's hard to say for sure," he frankly admitted. "I'm a wise enough man to know that I do not totally understand the female psyche all of the time."

She nodded in approval. "Good for you. But I'm sure you can read her distress fairly well. According to her, you can do everything and anything with prowess."

He cleared his throat uncomfortably. "She does ramble on."

She laughed indulgently. "We all need a hero."

"I'm counting on it, Karen."

Her breath lodged in her throat as the meaning of his words sank in. How could this wonderful man still be on the loose? Especially with all the beautiful nymphs frolicking around here?

They walked in a companionable silence the remainder of the way. Ross followed Walt's trek of the past two nights, unlocking a back service door to the hotel, ushering her inside with a hand on her arm.

Karen, of course, was trained to take good care of herself, had guarded her share of celebrities in Las Vegas. Still, she was impressed with the safety measures taken with the entertainers in Ross's employ. The onsite ones were always accompanied back here. The others were escorted to their residences.

Ross took care of his own in a very flattering way. Karen was quickly growing into his most dazzled admirer, second only to Wendy!

Two turns down the long hushed hallways brought them to the employee wing. Karen had her key in hand as they paused in front of her suite. Ross noted this with a wince. "Trying to give me the bum's rush, songbird?"

Her surprised laughter was musical. "Trying to rush you inside."

"Oh, well, let me show you the way!" Ross swiftly and smoothly traded the flower box for the key. Karen waited patiently while he opened the door and switched on the alcove light. She sailed inside with the flowers while he resecured the dead bolt. "I hope you keep this tight," he lectured, giving the knob a test tug. "I—" He whirled around at the sound of running water. She wasn't even listening!

"Karen!" He strode into the kitchenette, where she was already in stocking feet, arranging the flowers into a tall crystal vase. "It's important that you—" He paused in midspeech at the sight of her beguiling face.

"Oh, Ross, don't worry. I know all about security," she pleaded softly. "I don't even want to talk about it. Not right now, anyway." She raised a rose to her face, rubbing the half-open velvet bud to her cheek. "It was so sweet of you to give me these flowers. They mean more to me tonight...than you could possibly ever know."

"You deserve them, honey," he intoned, closing the space between them. "You sounded so good. So much stronger."

Karen drew a doubtful pout. "And how would you know?"

"I caught a few of the numbers," he confessed, taking the single stem from her hand. He stuffed it into the vase with the impatience of a child jamming a straw into a malt. "I covered a lot of territory tonight, but I managed to pop in and out on my protégée."

"I believe these new high marks smack more than a little of blind favoritism," she suggested.

"Maybe calling yours an irresistible magic would be fair middle ground," he bartered. "But you improve with every note. Trust me."

The request for trust was laden with meaning and promise. She took a shaky breath, trying to focus in the dizzy spin of circumstances. Her enchantment with Wendy, her attraction to him, all with a backdrop of applause from an adulating audience. It was like a fairy tale come to life. And the prince of the palace was contemplating his next move.... His eyes steamed like coffee, burning into hers with a raw desire.

With a mighty groan, Ross gathered her into his arms, shucking the shawl from her bare shoulders.

Winding her hands around his neck, she tipped up her mouth in hungry offering. He dipped down to kiss her with a leisurely, gentle sweetness.

A shiver of delight coursed down her spine as he ever so gently explored her face with his mouth, nibbling on her earlobes, her throat. It was difficult to believe that only last week, tending to the weakening Irene, she'd been swimming in despair, mourning the impending loss of her beloved aunt.

But just as that door closed, another was magically opening....

All because Irene had mustered the courage to tug it ajar with her last ounce of strength. Karen wanted to believe that Irene had felt an impetuous rush of sentiment and profound regret over giving Baby Bradford up for adoption. It helped with the healing.

As did Ross and Wendy. Despite the newness of their relationship, there seemed to be such a seamless connection between everyone involved. Wendy carried so many Bradford traits, and so much of her personality was honed by this caring, loving, ridiculously over-protective father, whose only sin seemed to be loving his child too much.

The pressure of Ross's mouth was increasing as his kisses moved down the delicate column of her throat.

Karen couldn't help wishing that Ross loved her too much, in the lush, crazed way only two adults could understand and appreciate.

A flame of hope for some kind of future with him was beginning to burn bright and steady in her heart.

Another more urgent fire burned lower, making her hips heavy with an intensifying heat.

The idea of Ross filling her magnified the aching emptiness inside her.

And he was going to do it.

As his gaze delved deeply into hers, she found her own hungry passions mirrored there. It drove home the certainty of his amatory intent. This was not going to end with a few strokes and embraces.

With a languid sigh, Karen swayed into him, capturing his mouth all over again. He grew forceful, crushing her against his length, his hands greedily skimming her body.

The smooth silver fabric was metallic cool beneath his fingers, a shocking counterpoint to her hot, exposed skin.

Karen gasped with him as his fingertips roamed her dress and creamy shoulders. A deep curl of fire spiraled up from the pit of her belly.

It was really happening. Just the way she'd dreamed it might.

"Ross . . ." His name erupted in a moaning plea. "I want you so much."

"I want you too, honey," he admitted huskily. "But I also want you to know how special I think you are. This sort of intimate escort home isn't a habit with me."

Tenderness suffused her face. "I know it isn't, Ross. It's plain to see just how things are."

He surveyed her features, marveling over every contour. "You are so lovely on stage. I—I was almost afraid to speak to you at first," he confided with awe, "afraid you'd break the spell. But you're everything I hoped you might be." He shook his head in wonderment. "Even better up close."

Karen's heart hammered hard over the revelation. He was sinking right along with her into an emotional meltdown.

"I know. I feel the same," she blurted out throatily. "It's like a wonderful dream."

"Let me love you, Karen," he coaxed, his voice caressing her name.

The request was a courtesy. Her long, tan fingers were already fumbling with the knot of his tie.

And he was already tugging at her back zipper, sliding it open along her spine with a seductive, scratching sound. Though he was quaking with desire, he took great care with her gown, peeling it away from her skin with gentle hands, dropping to his knee to spread the pooled fabric so she could step out of it.

Karen found the gesture tantalizingly gallant. She braced her hands on his shoulders and lifted one foot, then the other, out of the circle of the gown.

Ross remained frozen on his knee at eye level with her hips for a long moment. Karen's lean, supple body was on breathtaking display, in nothing more than a pair of glossy tights. The effect was dazzlingly erotic, her nest of pale curls crushed behind the sheer mesh barrier.

With a groan of wonder, he traced his fingers over the captivating triangle.

The scraping sensations made by his blunt fingernails caused her to shudder, bringing a musky moistness to her tender opening. Her scent permeated his breathing space. He inhaled longingly. The garment he'd been cradling fell to the floor with a rustle as his hands jumped to her hipbones to explore her nyloncovered legs, then reached back to the curve of her bottom to massage her taut flesh with his strong, nimble fingers.

"Exquisite . . ." he rasped.

"Oh, Ross," she gently scoffed, "with all the beauties around here—"

"Hush now." His order was a rough, impatient whisper as he gently began to unroll her hose before tossing them onto the dress. "I'm a man who knows exactly what he wants. Who wants to give you whatever you want."

Karen stood over him, fingering his soft dark hair with an endearing sigh. "I'd like to finish removing your tie. For beginners."

He straightened up in one fluid motion, his expression shadowed with passion and amusement. "Your wish is my command."

And he meant it. He remained loosely passive as she began to take off his clothing. He was as casual as a model on a runway, aside from the rock-hard arousal straining his blue bikini briefs.

His powerful frame tingled with a new awareness as Karen took her own sweet time removing his underwear, running her thumbs along the elastic, teasing his rigid flesh with flicking fingertips, feeding off his trembling pleasure with sultry noises. It seemed like an eternity before she peeled the last scrap of cotton from his skin.

Ross was astonished by her boldness, her coyness. She was a decade younger than him, but confident in her moves. As she wound her arms around his neck, her eyes were shimmering with the knowledge and anticipation of a wanton wildcat. A slow grin of delight split his face. This was an added bonus in his mind, one which only encouraged him to initiate more adventurous play....

Karen opened her mouth to savor the taste of his hungry, demanding kiss. She sensed a new drive behind his methods now, a more ruthless approach than yesterday's tentative experimentation.

She cried out in delight when, with an effortless sweep, he lifted her off the floor into the cradle of his arms and headed for the bedroom.

The peach satin spread had already been turned down by the maid, and the bedside lamp glowed invitingly. He eased them both between the blue designer sheets and against a bank of pillows, his powerful limbs covering her liquid length.

Karen's hands stole to his chest, and she ran her fingernails through his mat of springy black hair, scraping over the surface of his flat brown nipples.

"Honey..." A rough shudder shook him.

"I've barely touched you," she breathed back with a lazy grin.

"Not so," he protested hoarsely. "I've already played this whole scene through once before. Last night in my dreams..."

A testimonial to die for. His words made her ache all the more for fulfillment. But the building tension was so sweet. She wanted him, but she wanted it to last.

Ross pressed his solid body deeper into her soft length, raking his fingers through her tumbling curtain of satin blond hair, showering kisses along her throat. He reached behind her head, pulling the pillows free of the headboard. Karen let him have his way, shifting cooperatively as he worked to press the pillows behind her shoulder blades, making her back arch and giving an upward thrust to her high, firm breasts.

"You do have vivid dreams," she gasped, tipping her head back over the edge of the pillows.

"Mmm . . ." He sat up to straddle her at the navel, gently caressing her creamy swells of flesh. Through an erotic haze, he found himself oddly touched by the white bikini lines slicing across her skin. Bare breasts and even tans were commonplace among stage entertainers. It was another exception in Karen's case, another mysterious facet of her personality.

Modest in public. Abandoned in a secluded tryst. She was loose and languid beneath him, enjoying his stroking with closed eyes and a dreamy smile.

His lovemaking gradually grew more demanding. With a gentle pinch to her nipple, he closed over it with his mouth. The suckling pull, the motion of his tongue drew the small dark circle to a hot, hard point of fire. Karen's fingers raked through his hair, urging him on to the other breast with moans of encouragement.

Ross reveled in her glorious torment, flicking, nibbling her buds to an achingly turgid state.

"Oh, Ross!" Her breathing was labored and her color high when he drew his mouth to hers to share her own salty sweetness. Her fingers stole down his ribs, his smooth, flat stomach, scraping through his coarse hairs, capturing his erection in the circle of her fingers.

"Ahh..." A groan of pleasure tore from his throat as she stroked and squeezed with a knowing touch. Concerned with his store of stamina, he began to think about the practicalities of protection. "Karen, honey, are you taken care of?"

She blinked to focus, picking up on his meaning. "Yes. It doesn't seem necessary a lot of the time, but it's a habit I fell into."

Irene had made certain Karen had birth control pills after the pregnancy. She'd expressed her disapproval over young, irresponsible sex, but had supplied the safeguard just the same.

How ironic that Karen needed them now, making love to the only father her child would ever know!

Ross was watching her closely, his eyes full of hope and lust and perhaps just a little uncertainty. He so openly wanted a merging of minds as well as bodies.

Someday soon, Ross, she silently promised. You and I will have no more secrets between us.

Ever so gently, Ross turned her over on the pillows, stretching out over her slender, supple back. She trembled in ecstasy as his fingers stole around to her nest of curls, then down to her thighs, prying, probing, pleasing.

Moments stretched into longer moments as they indulged in searing, shuddering play. Ross's control stretched like an elastic band, way beyond his known limits. He'd forgotten how good the good thing could be, what it was like to explore and enjoy with genuine passion.

When they did eventually discover they were on the brink of shattering, Karen eased beneath him without hesitation. Her thighs were trembling and he had to wrap them around his hips, hold them steady so he could enter her.

Three slicing thrusts was all it took to rocket them over the edge. He went taut, arching against her, sharing a mutual vivid explosion. They slowly sank into the pulsing waves, clinging to one another with short ragged breaths.

They collapsed together on the collection of strewn pillows. Spent and sated.

Ross reached out, pulling her head into the crook of his arm. "Oh, honey, where does an angel like you come from?"

It took all her self-control not to tell him.

# 9

KAREN ROUTINELY SURVIVED on six hours of sleep a night, so despite her rendezvous with Ross, she awoke at seven o'clock Monday morning.

She struggled to sit up in the center of the vast king-size bed, flooded with an overwhelming sense of abandonment.

How unexpected. And how silly. Her rich blond hair tumbled over her bare shoulders as she gave her head a self-chiding shake. She certainly was accustomed to waking up alone. She was single. And a solitary cop, who, if not officially married to her job, was certainly seriously engaged. Of course she'd had her share of affairs over the past several years, but had never even been tempted to share her quarters with anyone.

But Ross had left an indelible mark on her. One night in his arms and she was hooked in an exciting, but alarmingly vulnerable way.

He'd been reluctant to leave her, but had gently explained that it was his habit to awaken in his own bedroom whenever possible for Wendy's sake. It gave their life a sense of continuity and the security Wendy deserved.

How could any mother argue with such a compassionate policy?

Karen's impulsive nature had spurred her to launch questions at him as he'd dressed to leave. Did they breakfast together? What time did Wendy leave for school?

He'd wearily, but good-naturedly given her a run-down on their rituals. Most mornings were rushed—coffee, cereal, brief conversation. Wendy headed out the front door to school and Ross made tracks for his office in the casino.

In short, he hadn't invited her to join them.

Karen rubbed her eyes with a self-recriminating groan. Did he think her mad? Nosy, compulsive, starved for attention?

What a disastrous thought!

It was so difficult to throttle back, behave like a moderately interested friend. But in her own defense, she had just one short week to absorb it all, give Wendy a boost. She would have to push a bit, take some risks.

With that reinforcement, she flung back the covers and scrambled out of bed. She'd have to hurry if she wanted to accidentally run into Wendy while out for a brisk morning jog.

Karen set out fifteen minutes later, dressed in a bold blue-and-green nylon running suit, a white terry visor on her head. The hotel was located near the front of the resort, and the Chandlers' retreat was deliberately set way back on the property, with a separate private road leading out to the town's main arteries.

It didn't take long to make her way toward their red-wood chalet sheltered in the pines. And luck was with her. Wendy was standing at the curb, dressed in a pink culotte dress that Karen had seen in her closet yesterday. A white spring jacket hung loosely on her narrow shoulders and a denim knapsack was slung on her back.

"Hey, Wendy!" she called out, closing in on her with long, even strides.

Her daughter's first day of school, from her own unique perspective anyway.

"Hi, Karen!"

Karen hopped the curb, jogging in place for several seconds to wind down on the lush green boulevard.

"Gee, I never expected to see you this morning," Wendy exclaimed in candid delight. "Most of the entertainers around here sleep in pretty late."

"I only need several hours," Karen explained breathlessly.

Her daughter's eyes sparkled in rivalry with the bright cobalt sky. "I keep telling Dad that's all I need, but he doesn't believe me. Maybe you could talk to him. There's some TV shows on later at night that I'd really like to see—"

"Whoa!" Karen raised her hands, her brows jumping beneath the rim of her visor. "Growing girls need their rest."

"Yeah, right," the youngster grumbled. "Maybe I just won't help you get that permanent singing job," she threatened, her eyes still twinkling.

"Now, Wendy, I told you I don't want Tiffany's job."

"Well, you should," Wendy insisted on a whine. "I want you to stay around."

Karen's heart swelled with pleasure. "You do?"

"Sure. We're friends, aren't we?"

"Yes, of course!"

"I don't have many good friends," Wendy confided in complaint.

She had mentioned that the other day at the chalet. Of course, the child couldn't possibly know that Karen had been absorbing her every word, storing them away in her memory bank for review. "What about all the girls at school?" she asked gently.

Wendy's chin wobbled. "They don't like me much."

"Maybe they just don't know you," Karen speculated, recognizing her chance to voice her opinions. "You seem rather isolated here at the resort."

"I'd like to see them more, but they're jealous of what I have," the girl rushed on defensively. "I can't help it if Dad's rich."

"I know the tough spot you're in," Karen assured her. "I sometimes had trouble making friends."

Wendy's eyes grew round. "You? Why didn't they like you?"

Karen smiled wanly. "For a lot of different reasons. I didn't have the kind of house where they could come to hang out, or have a lot of nice clothes to wear." Karen sighed as the vivid memories caused her a niggle of pain. "The thing is, I also was set apart and know exactly how it feels."

"I try to be like them," Wendy lamented. "But it's so hard. I've tried to talk to Dad about it, but he just doesn't get it."

"He must be trying. He's throwing your birthday party."

"Poor old guy. He does his best. He is the best! But . . ." She faltered as she wrestled with her frustrations and loyalties. "He treats me like a baby sometimes. And he doesn't understand about being a girl."

"I suppose not."

"He thinks Nanny Grethal should be able to help me out just because she's a lady. But she doesn't know what I'm talking about, either!"

Karen couldn't help but chuckle. How could Ross be so naive? Nanny Grethal was from a completely different world. "Well, it's tough for older people to keep current."

"Yeah! That's what I mean!"

Karen bit her lip. There had to be some role models around this big place, women who could guide Wendy in her friendships, help her change her petulant attitude. "What about Dinah?" she asked with inspiration.

Wendy shrugged. "She's okay. She likes to help. But she's really busy and isn't as great as you."

Karen closed her eyes for a brief moment to control her elation. The tug between them was so strong! She saw so much family discord on the job. And the talk shows were full of disastrous birth parent and child reunions. But she and Wendy were clicking in such an easy, natural way. As if it was meant to be . . .

"We'll talk more about this after school," Karen promised as a yellow school bus materialized on the winding mountain road off in the distance. "Your ride's coming—"

"Oh, that's not my ride," Wendy returned matter-of-factly. "I don't take the bus."

Karen's jaw slacked. "Not ever?"

"Dad doesn't let me," she explained. "He has a driver take me."

Another wedge between Wendy and her peers. Karen was still absorbing this news when a long white limousine oozed up the street from the direction of the hotel.

"See, here's my ride," Wendy chirped, stepping closer to the curb.

A limo? For school? What a symbol to flaunt at the beginning of each morning! "Wendy, I wonder if this kind of ride might just intimidate your friends," she ventured, struggling to keep the disapproval and awe from her tone.

Wendy was torn between agitation and uncertainty. "I don't know!" she finally blurted out. "Dad says it's for my own good."

"A trip on the bus might be interesting," Karen suggested. "Everybody talks, laughs, gets warmed up for the day."

The driver had stepped out onto the street and was opening the rear door for Wendy.

"Got to go," she said, giving Karen a swift hug.

Karen closed her eyes, squeezing her hard. "See you later."

She watched the vehicle silently slide away like a long white cat.

KAREN WANDERED the plush carpeted floors of her suite for thirty minutes that afternoon before mustering the courage to call Franklin Stewart's law office and face a less comfortable kind of music. As she anticipated, Justine's reaction was in swift counterpoint to her maudlin mood.

"It's about time you called, lady-sings-the-blues!"

Karen crossed her legs on the freshly made bed, setting the phone on her ankles. "It's only Monday, Justine!"

"The judge is an old man. Every hour has been an eternity for him."

"Dinah told you yesterday that I'm doing fine."

"Too fine, it sounds like."

Karen rolled her eyes to the ceiling. "You are the one who set this up, the one who encouraged me to move in close."

"I didn't mean cozy close," Justine hissed softly over the wire.

"I take it Stew doesn't know the details," Karen surmised with relief.

"Of course he doesn't! He can't take another shock to his system. Just tell me, Karen, what can you be dreamin' of?"

The works. Karen was beginning to dream of forevers. She took a breath to steady herself. "I am in control of this situation."

Justine made a rude noise.

"This is my life," Karen objected.

"Your life is on hold right now. You've stepped into Wendy's life. You're supposed to be a guest, an observer."

"I'm doing my best."

"The best a mother can do is to step back behind her child, put her first always. It's the way it's done. The way it should be."

Karen knew Justine had a right to spout that lecture. She practiced what she preached, devoting herself to her own two lively sons.

"You simply can't put your needs ahead of Wendy's, hon."

"I wouldn't!"

"Not deliberately, of course," Justine soothed, backing down under Karen's hurt tone. "So, what's she like?"

An affectionate smile curved Karen's lips. "Beautiful and healthy. Spoiled and sheltered. But the mother is a disaster, Justine. Wendy's shortcomings are due to her environment."

"I can hear our Miz Fix-it talkin'."

"I can't help caring," Karen confessed in an excited rush. "And she cares about me, Justine. I mean, really cares."

"I'm happy for you," Justine assured her in a stronger, more formal voice. "The judge is standing by now, anxious for a word. Oh, yes, and Chief Bradley called this morning. He'd like to touch base with you about a burglary you investigated last month. I think there's a hearing tomorrow. He knows you're supposed to be incognito, resting, but he'd like a minute of your time."

"All right, I'll give him a call."

"Thanks. Here's the judge."

Karen respectfully absorbed his displeasure over her decision not to consult him, but managed to steer clear of any real issues. Of course, he wanted to hear all about Wendy and there she could oblige.

"Remember to keep looking forward," he advised as her voice grew husky.

He so wanted her to admit that Irene had done right. But she just couldn't bring herself to do that. "I am focused on the future, Stew," she insisted after a short pause. "No one knows better than a scrapper like me how important our tomorrows are."

Karen hastily made her goodbyes soon after that. She understood Stew's concern, but he was out of this phase of things. He and Irene had handled her past as they'd thought best. But the future he'd spoken of was rightfully in her hands alone.

Slipping into the fun vacationer mode that would be expected of her at the station, she dialed the chief's number.

ROSS WENT ABOUT HIS Monday routine as usual, but Karen was never far from his mind. Last night's lovemaking had been so exciting, so fulfilling. The uninhibited intensity of it took him way back to his young bachelor days before Margo, when he and Ron had

trotted the globe, looking for adventure and very often finding it.

Karen seemed the woman of his dreams with the siren's lure to a better state of being.

It was as though she rode a magic carpet and offered
to take him along for the ride. And he suspected that
last night had only been a test spin....

All his initial vibrations concerning her seemed on
the mark. He'd had damn good reason to be a little
shook up over her impact as a songstress. It had been
just a spellbinding sample.

But he had to tread cautiously. He and Wendy were
in this together.

Ross had been meaning to check up on Wendy after
school and was surprised to spot her in the hotel pool
as he emerged from a meeting with the managers.

"Hey, Dad! Watch this!" Wendy waved to Ross from
the diving board, then plunged headfirst into the water with a quick, clean slice. Ross gave her the thumbs-
up signal as she resurfaced, then wandered over to the
cushioned chaise lounge where Nanny Gee, in her plaid
housedress and rubber-soled shoes, was stretched out
with her knitting, looking comically out of place
among the oiled vacationers.

"Why is she swimming here, when we have a per-
fectly fine pool over at the house?" he inquired with a
small, bewildered smile.

Grethal gave her yarn a yank, clicking away on her
afghan project with a smooth, unruffled rhythm. "Ask
her, *Vater*. Ask her why I must postpone my beef stew
supper."

"Did you like me?" Wendy scurried up behind them,
her bare feet pattering on the concrete, her thin, wispy

frame and lime green tank suit dripping with chlorinated water.

"A rubber cap would give you more momentum," he teased, tweaking her nose.

She rewarded him with a wiggle that sent droplets of water at his tan twill slacks and white muslin shirt.

"Hey, knock it off! I have an image to maintain!"

"I could just hug you!" she threatened with a playful lilt.

He reared back in mock fear. "Save it for a very dry later."

"Okay."

"What are you doing here, honey? Waiting for me?"

"No," she blurted back, causing him to wince in disappointment. "I'm waiting for Karen. She's still rehearsing with the band, and I want her to swim with me."

"Does she know?"

"No," she admitted in a smaller voice.

Ross released an exasperated sigh. "Wendy..."

"She said she'd see me after school," she assured him.

"When did she say that?" He arched a confused brow.

"She was out jogging this morning and she stopped to talk to me."

A secret smile touched his mouth. "I'm surprised that she was up and about that early."

"She said she only needs a few hours' sleep a night. I told you some people are that way."

"I hope this isn't a campaign for a later curfew," he warned.

"Oh, no. Karen says I need a lot of rest because I'm growing."

"But that's what I've been saying all along!"

"Sure, Dad. But she knows so much about beauty tips and stuff."

"Glad we're all on the same side," he mumbled with mock relief.

"I guess I'm glad you showed up, though," she decided, "because I want to talk to you about something else."

"Oh. All right." Ross turned around to survey the cluster of deck chairs and pulled a dry one up beside Grethal's lounge.

Wendy gingerly perched herself at her nanny's feet, sending a sprinkle of water over the old woman's shoes.

Grethal shifted her feet with a sigh. "Tell him and get it over with."

"Dad, I want to try riding the bus to school."

"What!"

"Karen thinks I might fit in better with the other kids if I take the bus. And you know it might work. I'd be in on all the things they say before school. Part of the action."

"No, Wendy, no," he sputtered in surprise. "That's never been a debatable issue."

"But Karen says—"

"I don't care what she says or thinks about the matter." Ross balled his hands on his thighs, his expression smoldering. "It's an impossible request."

"You're impossible, Dad!" Wendy jumped up and hovered over him with her hands on her soaking hips.

Ross regarded her incredulously. "Wendy!"

"Such a way to talk," Grethal clucked.

"I want to try new things, Dad. It's unfair if you say no."

His gaze sharpened. "Did Karen put those words in your mouth?"

"No," she denied with a thrust of her small chin. "That's what I say."

Since when? Ross absorbed her defensive snap like a blow. He carefully flexed his hands, struggling to keep his voice steady. "I am your parent and I want to keep this sort of thing between the two of us."

Wendy gasped in exaggerated mortification. "Even if she has a great idea?"

Ross faltered for a brief moment, unnerved by his own woman-child and extremely annoyed with the woman goading her on. One way or the other, Karen was undoubtedly behind this. Wendy was in the fifth grade and had never before challenged her mode of transportation.

"This subject is closed," he declared adamantly, ris-ing to his feet. "And I want you to head back to the house."

"But Karen—"

"She isn't expecting you poolside," he stated firmly. "You didn't make any definite plans."

"You want to keep me away from her now, don't you?"

Ross sighed, reminding himself that Wendy had re-ally done nothing wrong. "What I really want is my Monday night stew. If you tie up Nanny Gee over here, she can't prepare it. All right?"

"Okay," she begrudgingly relented. "Whatever you say, Dad."

Hah! he fumed in silent despair. Those days would soon be a sweet, distant memory.

Ross helped the pair gather their stuff together and hailed a young male attendant to drive them home in a cart. He ran a hand through his hair with helpless frus-tration as they exited the pool area. When had Wendy begun to self-consciously tug her swimsuit over her hips and do shy double takes at the young men on his staff?

He couldn't stop the milestones, he understood that. But he couldn't help taking a new look at Karen from a different, more objective angle. What were her motives? She'd seeped into so many areas of their life. Her presence had been so pleasurable up till now that he hadn't analyzed it in earnest.

But he would do so in the future. He would slow things down between them. He would take a keener, calmer look at his new songbird.

"SHAME ON YOU, Ross Chandler!" Dinah shouted, barreling into her employer's office without invitation.

It was Wednesday morning and Ross was in conference with David behind his paneled walls. Walls that were normally respected as private.

"Didn't your mother teach you how to knock?"

"Didn't your nanny teach you how to treat a lady?" she sassed back.

Ross leaned back in his spring-loaded chair away from his paper-strewn desk, drilling Dinah with his most tyrannical glare. "We're doing some financial reports for the IRS. So unless this place is on fire, I suggest you hightail it out of here."

David rose from his chair, hiding a smile behind a cough. "We're really finished here, boss. I'll have someone type up a cover letter and get back to you."

Ross glared at his stout, middle-aged assistant as he collected the paperwork and stuffed it into a file folder.

"Thanks a lot, Dave."

The older man's round face split into a grin. "Don't mention it."

Ross watched him leave, shutting the door firmly behind him.

"Why do I feel like my inner circle is in some sort of conspiracy?"

"Because we are." Dinah dropped into Dave's vacated chair, raiding the jelly-bean jar on the desktop. "So why have you been avoiding Karen?"

He waved a dismissive hand. "I've been tied up."

"Too tied up to pick up the phone? I know she can't get through to you." She popped some candy into her mouth with an accusatory glare. "And I know that Wendy wanted to swim with her the other day and you axed the idea. Face it, Ross. This whole affair has been played out for all of us to see."

Ross rubbed his face, groaning. "Great."

"That's all you can say?"

"Look, I didn't realize that withdrawing a step for such a short span of time was going to cause a ruckus." He sighed through his teeth. "Does she know I sent Wendy away from the pool?"

The trace of concern on his face slowed her down. "No, I don't think so. Wendy told me herself."

"I suppose Wendy told you about the bus-ride deal, too."

"Yes...."

He wagged a finger at her. "I won't have that kind of interference, Dinah."

"I understand," she hastily assured him. "But you can't expect Karen to comprehend any of this."

"It's only been a couple of days!" he roared.

Dinah shook her red head at him in disbelief. "It isn't the amount of time. It's the timing! You seduce her, then you back off. Without a single word. After a whirlwind pickup. With everyone watching."

"Guess I wasn't looking at it from that angle," he admitted slowly. "I've got my own troubles, my own concerns, to think about right now."

"Don't try to pass yourself off as some sort of modern-day Socrates," she hooted. "You've hit a speed bump in this fling of yours and you're pouting like an adolescent."

"That's a fine diagnosis!"

Dinah sat up stiffly, tossing several black jelly beans back into the jar. "Look, you don't have a lot of time to make this thing with her fly!"

"It's my palace and I'll pout if I want to," he returned with a false smile.

She wagged a finger at him. "You aren't going to slough me off that easily. You finally lower your defenses to let somebody in and you jump back the minute you're peeved."

Ross leaned forward, placing his palms on the desk. "Look, you're partly right."

"Damn right I'm right!" she bellowed.

"But considering the fact that Wendy is in the middle of this, and that Karen is so temporary—"

"She doesn't live on the moon, dummy. She's as close as Las Vegas!"

"Your sensitivity concerning my reservations is remarkable," he returned sarcastically. "But I think a little caution is in order here. Her overwhelming interest in Wendy is on the one hand a wonderful thing, but on the other it's also risky."

"Why don't you ask Wendy if she thinks it's worth the risk," Dinah challenged sweetly.

He made a careless gesture. "We know I don't have to."

"She is so good for Wendy, Ross!"

And she was good for him, as well. Dinah was right. He took business risks every day. He'd never see a relationship through if he didn't take some chances.

"I'll speak to her," he promised.

"Don't blow up now, will you?"

"No, I won't blow up."

"It would be a very unpleasant sight," she informed him airily, rising from her chair. "You might want to run through your apology a few times, to hit just the right expression of sincerity."

Apology? She always knew just how to get under his skin. Ross slanted her a mocking smile, deciding to rehearse his eloquence on her. "You can get the hell out of here. Before I wring your neck."

Dinah strolled to the door, turning to form an *0* with her fingers. "Perfect Miss Manners pomp and tone, boss. But soften the message just a teensy."

# 10

ROSS EXITED HIS OFFICE and headed into his vast control room several minutes later, tugging his striped tie into place over his pale blue shirt.

He stopped short before Dinah, who was standing in his path with a cup of nickels.

"What's this for?" he demanded as she nudged the cup against his chest.

"For Karen," she anxiously explained. "Use it as an icebreaker."

His forehead furrowed in confusion. "Is this one of your tricks?"

"No!" she denied in affront. "She's downstairs, at one of the slots."

Ross turned to David, who was seated at the intricate control panel keeping tabs on the room below.

David nodded in affirmation, pointing up at the wall of television screens. "She's in living color on seven, Ross."

Ross wandered over, standing behind David's shoulder to study the row of nickel slots on view. Sure enough, Karen was down there, feeding a machine five coins at a time. She had a fresh springtime prettiness about her, dressed in a cherry red tank top and black belted shorts, her golden mane tied back in a sleek ponytail. She was animated, as well, chatting with the players on her right and left.

"Ah, I love that easily approachable kind of dame," David commented lightly.

Ross glared down at his bald spot. "Fine remark from a happily married man."

"Nah, I was just smart enough to find one of my own."

"This really smells like a setup," Ross uttered in suspicion, looking around the room.

Dinah fluttered her russet lashes. "Oh, don't all the new resort employees get a certificate for a complimentary cup of coins in the Sultan's Room?"

Ross's mouth pulled into a phony smile. "Not that I know of."

"Well, they should," the group of fifteen employees chorused in the background.

"Oh, give me that cup!" Ross growled in surrender. "And don't even think of watching us on that monitor."

A round of denials followed him out the door.

Ross Chandler certainly stood out in a crowd.

Karen caught his advance out of the corner of her eye. He was incredibly handsome in his tan linen suit and blue shirt, poised and sure as he prowled through the bustling room.

And his eyes were pinned on her. She turned just a fraction too far in his direction, giving her awareness away. He promptly captured her gaze, holding it fast with his own. The thin link between them grew spine-tinglingly tangible in the moments to follow.

Her heart was hammering with anticipation, and a new hope.

Maybe he hadn't been avoiding her after all....

"Hi, songbird."

His voice was surprisingly husky as he eased up behind her. She returned his smile rather tentatively.

"Hello, Ross."

"These are for you." He offered her the new cup of coins.

"For me?" she breathlessly teased, slipping it inside her empty cup. "Really? How lovely."

They shared a laugh, shaking off the discomfort of reconnecting.

"I hope it doesn't seem stingy of me. I could've filled it with say, quarters."

Karen lifted her smooth shoulders beneath her tank top. "Another cup of nickels is fine. I'm not much of a gambler, really. Moderation in all things is my motto."

"In most areas, perhaps," he corrected with a sensual curl to his mouth.

Karen could feel a flush heating her cheeks as she thought back on their satisfying tryst. "You know, Ross, I thought that you might be avoiding me."

Ross sighed hard, propping his forearm against the machine in an effort to get closer and to obstruct the view of the security cameras.

"I'd really like to talk to you."

"Well, I happen to be very free at the moment," she lilted in invitation.

Ross skimmed his chin with his fingers. "It's so hard in this atmosphere," he finally said under his breath. "Let's go have some lunch."

"If you like."

With a casual arm looped around her shoulders, he ushered her through the crowd and out the grand entrance.

They stood outside on the pyramid-shaped staircase for a moment as Karen stuffed her cup of nickels into her tote. She looked around as she fumbled with the bag's zipper, absorbing the scenery. She wanted to remember the way the huge fountain fronting the casino glistened in the sunshine. The fresh smells of the freshly cut lawns, the cedars and pines.

She was storing it all up in her memory bank, along with every other word and event.

"Where to?" she asked brightly.

"How about my place."

"Oh. Okay."

They descended to the sidewalk, Ross's hand on her elbow. "Don't mind walking, do you? I could use some time outside."

"No, no, that's fine!" she assured him. "It isn't far."

He flashed her a thin smile. "Nobody knows that better than you do."

So her suspicions were true. He was angry about her homing in on Wendy the other day. It had taken all her willpower not to return today to see if the girl had taken her advice and hopped aboard the bus. But Karen had been cautious enough to look before she leapt. As the boys in the band had so wisely pointed out, the employees here lived a fishbowl existence. She would've been caught spying for sure and he would've been doubly infuriated with her!

She didn't want to put this budding relationship with him at risk. Ross was becoming far too special to her to be taken on only as the adoptive father of her child! Self-control was the answer. But it was the last thing she cared to practice with this dynamic man. Karen was falling hard for Ross Chandler. His abrupt withdrawal from her life had shaken her badly, had given her a lesson in the wisdom of temperance that a hundred lectures from Stew couldn't have accomplished!

"So, what have you been doing with yourself?" she asked brightly in an effort to draw him out of his distraught shell.

"Takes a lot of time and energy to keep this place going." They paused at the curb to allow a cart to pass them by.

"Be up-front with me, Ross. Please."

He looked around to meet her forthright gaze. Her leadoff made directness a lot easier. "I was upset to hear about your conversation with Wendy."

"About taking the school bus."

"Yes!"

"It was just a small suggestion," she assured him defensively.

"I realize that, Karen. But to me, it's more complex than that."

"How? Please explain."

They stepped off the curb and walked across the street. "The bus is fine for some of the children, I'm sure," he continued on. "Necessary. But only a percentage ride it."

She took long strides to keep up with him. "I thought it might help her blend in."

"I've never been totally honest with Wendy about why I have her driven to school in the limo. It's mainly a security measure. Just think of how it would affect the other students on the bus, if one day it was sideswiped or infiltrated because of us. And the weather up here is damn unpredictable at times. There are days when the roads are treacherous, slippery from a variety of storms."

"Oh..." Her voice trailed off as she absorbed the weight of his words.

"Riding the bus most likely was commonplace to you, but it simply isn't so around here. There are a lot of wealthy families living in this area, and they, too, drive their children to school."

"In ostentatious limos?" she challenged.

He flashed her a strained smile. "I don't know."

"A smaller company car would probably make far less of an entrance," she pressed. "You know, take some of the regality out of her arrival."

His profile softened as he pondered the idea. "It's worth a try." His chest rose and fell with a mighty sigh. "A small price for peace."

Karen felt a niggle of guilt over his open distress. He was no doubt feeling hopelessly outnumbered.

"Believe me, Ross, the last thing I want to do is undermine you. Or lead Wendy to believe that I'm the last word on what's best. It is natural for her to be hungry for female role models, though." She smiled affectionately. "I'm so flattered that she likes me."

Ross gritted his teeth, certain that he'd explode if he didn't confide his fears. "Karen, I feel as though the slats have been shoved out from under me all of a sudden."

"Over this?"

"Well, Wendy called me—impossible!"

"Oh, Daddy darling," she scoffed gently, reaching up to stroke his rigid jawline. "It's the rites of passage. The age."

"It's never happened before," he protested anxiously. "She always considered me the last word. Her hero. Now, I'm—impossible!" He spit out the word like the most heinous insult.

"Wendy is just eager to explore," Karen consoled him. "My different point of view is just a novelty. Lik all girls her age, she is full of all sorts of bold ideas a secret ambitions. She'll be struggling more and more. She'll be in a tug-of-war all the time, wanting your approval, then bucking your guidelines."

"So much to look forward to," he grumbled.

"You'll love it. Even when you hate it, you'll love it."

"Hope you're right."

"Now tell me, boss man, just where did that first cup of nickels come from? I know a setup when I see one."

"You walked right into it anyway," he noted with a gleam of amusement.

"Of course! I wanted to be trapped all over again!"

He slackened his stride, wound an arm around her waist and explained how Dinah had played matchmaker, luring her to the Sultan's Room with the free offer.

They were both laughing as they entered the chalet. Ross's expression turned to one of tender consternation when they found Nanny Gee running a carpet sweeper over the huge living room rug in front of the stone fireplace.

"Grethal, how many times have I told you to leave the cleaning to the housekeepers?"

Grethal didn't miss a sweeping stroke as she turned her head to reply. "Nothing else to do when Wendy's away."

Ross threw his hands into the air. "Relax! Sit by the pool. Stretch out on the sofa with some magazines. Watch TV."

Her tsk was scolding and dismissing.

Ross put a halting hand on the sweeper handle. "Take a break. It's lunchtime."

Grethal sighed, pushing some gray wisps of hair off her temples. "All right. I'll take a break and make you lunch."

"I could fix us something," Karen promptly offered as Grethal bustled her way toward the open kitchen area.

"It's no use," Ross remarked loudly. "She runs this place single-handedly."

"I have some chicken salad for sandwiches right here in the refrigerator," she called back over her shoulder. "And the romaine lettuce you like so well. Just relax," she said chortling. "Stretch out. Watch TV."

Ross threw up his hands again as his own advice was tossed back at him. "Why do I still have the compulsion to obey her?" he whispered.

"Oh, I imagine it's an automatic reflex, ingrained with years of practice. I, too—" Karen halted in mid-sentence, breaking off the intended candid reference to Irene poised on her lips.

"What were you going to say?" he demanded eagerly.

"It's really nothing," she said with a fluid shrug.

But it was a big something to him. He eyed her keenly for a long moment, wondering. He wasn't sure to what degree or why, but again he felt that she was deliberately holding out on him.

Admittedly he was guarded himself. But it was his nature. Such chariness just didn't seem to suit her. She radiated with spontaneity. Except when speaking about herself. She was so damn cryptic with her admissions. Cryptic and clever. He was doing all the talking in a relationship for the first time in his life! She finagled facts out of him like no one else ever!

It was time for some turnabout treatment.

For as strong as his libido was calling out to him for a second lovemaking match, his yearnings for information, understanding, were even deeper right now.

He would've pinned her down right then and there if the doorbell hadn't chimed. Ross made reluctant strides to the entrance to find Dinah and Chef Fellman from his catering staff on the stoop.

"What? Why?" He stared at them in open disappointment.

"Who'd have ever guessed you'd bring her back here?" Dinah squeaked in bleak disbelief.

Ross smiled thinly. "I live here."

Dinah sighed hard. "Well, I'm afraid we're expected." She used the clipboard in her hand to sweep Ross aside. "C'mon, Fellman."

The small wiry chef flashed Ross an apologetic look as he passed.

"Grethal?" Dinah called out, waving to Karen, who was perched on the arm of a low leather chair near the hearth.

Nanny Gee emerged from the kitchen, wiping her hands on a dish towel, a warm greeting on her lips. *"Guten Tag."*

Ross pivoted in query. "What is this?"

"A meeting about Wendy's party," Dinah explained, making herself comfortable at the dining-room table.

"Oh, really?" Karen piped up.

Ross's ears picked up the far-too-interested pitch to her voice. With a swift motion, he drew her to her feet and steered her toward the kitchen.

Karen paused by the stove as he raced around the cheery room of stainless steel and earth-tone tiles. He was everywhere all at once, producing a wicker basket, a bottle of wine, utensils, chips, fruit.

"Ah, I believe we're outta here," she murmured with a knowing nod.

"Exactly. I'll just run upstairs to change clothes."

While he was away, Karen piled everything into the basket and put together Grethal's half-made chicken sandwiches.

Karen didn't realize how serious he was about distancing himself until he returned, dressed in a faded khaki-colored T-shirt and shorts and scuffed athletic shoes. Surely not an image he would ever show on the grounds.

He found some wax paper for the sandwiches. While she wrapped them, he made a quick call to David.

"Okay," he announced moments later, grabbing the handles of the basket. "We're all set."

She tried to pause at the dining-room table for a brief party update, but Ross kept her moving with a blanket farewell.

"You really want a clean getaway, don't you?" she retorted over her shoulder as he steered her out into the attached garage angled behind the house.

He paused, taking a deep breath. "Have to get you away. And only wheels will make it fast enough and far enough."

Karen gazed along the row of vehicles, from the Jeep to the white Buick Park Avenue to the navy Porsche. "Hey, your sports car's the same color as your underwear," she teased. "Any significance?"

He wiggled a brow, pressing the automatic garage door opener. "Let's take the silver Jeep and see if there's a pattern."

Ross wasted no time rolling off the property and up a winding mountain road. The Jeep had no topper and the wind hit them in steady hot gusts. Karen was glad she was dressed for it in her red tank and black shorts and comfortable shoes. She had the feeling, however, that nothing could've kept Ross from this trek right now. If she'd been wearing something formal, he'd have dressed her in some of his gear.

The road was a narrow two-lane blacktop and obviously required some skill to take with any speed. Ross maneuvered each curve and bump with familiar ease, making the ride quite smooth and pleasant.

They drove quite a spell over what seemed like endless miles of the same landscape. Vast green wilderness, thick forest terrain. Up, up to where the sky met the crown of mountains. Was he just driving to nowhere? she wondered. Was he so anxious to escape the invasive energy of his own resort?

It eventually became apparent, however, that he had a particular destination in mind. Along one of the bends an open bay appeared in the dense pines. Ross braked well ahead of the spot and eased off to the side. He stopped a good distance from the road and killed the engine.

"Why do I have the feeling you've done this before?"

His mouth twitched. "This is my special spot for meditation."

"New name for it."

"I'm serious," he insisted. "When I want to think, need some peace, I come up here."

Karen flashed him an endearing look. "You're a good man, Chandler." *Maybe too good.* She couldn't help the naughty niggle moving in from the corner of her mind—the cowardly wish that he had just brought her up here to seduce her. In the physical act of love, she could respond in total honesty and abandon. It was the conversations launched into unknown territory that left her guarded and awkward.

He wanted to know her better—every woman's wish. But each revelation she let slip was a risk. It was impossible to know what he'd been told at the time of the adoption. Surely the name Irene Bradford would ring a flurry of bells.

They climbed out of the Jeep, and Ross dug into the back seat for the basket and a blanket. Karen stood nearby with her hands in her pockets. Behind her calm smile, possibilities tumbled through her mind. What facts would be potential tip-offs? Her looks and her age seemed to roll off him. But it would only take one wrong step to arouse his suspicions. One pertinent fact to trigger a whole line of truths.

"You're thoughtful, songbird."

Karen blinked, smiling at Ross as he approached her with curiosity. "Just enjoying the scenery."

"Wait until you see my place," he tempted her with a wink.

Tossing the blanket over the basket, Ross offered Karen his free hand. Together they moved along a crude path through the trees. The towering pines offered shelter and shade and an occasional dapple of sunshine. They eventually reached a bright open clearing. They stood side by side for a silent moment, listening to the birds, the breeze and the ripple of a nearby mountain stream.

"How did you ever find this place, Ross?"

"Patience. Determination. Refusing to settle for anything less."

He was referring to her, as well. It was clearly imprinted in his hazy look.

"I love the way your eyes crinkle," she confessed, touching the spot with a tentative finger.

"I love learning about what you love," he murmured back.

His eyes gleamed with purpose, causing her heart to leap. Would he let her go without digging out every one of her secrets?

"Let's move closer to the stream," she suggested enthusiastically.

He watched her with an observant gleam. "Never been up to the mountains before, have you?"

She hadn't. Every kid in Nevada probably had at one time or another. But not her. There had never been anyone in her life remotely interested. He was waiting for an answer, so she sheepishly shook her head.

"Then you'll really remember, Karen," he said with pleasure. "Me. Everything. I like that idea a lot."

They spread out the blanket on the needle-cushioned ground.

"You bring Wendy up here?"

"Rarely," he replied with a trace of disappointment. "She's not much of a nature lover."

"Oh, maybe in time . . ."

"Sure, when some muscle-bound football jock wants to picnic," he retorted. "Then my bunny will be smelling the sweet air, gushing over the mountain streams."

Karen couldn't help laughing over his lament. "Life marches on."

He wore a dour look. "It does at that." He paused, fingering a pine needle. "So, where were we before our interruption back home?"

She wasn't fooled by his pensive pause. He was again homing in on her personal life.

"Oh, yeah. I was complaining about Grethal and you were about to top me."

"How about some wine?" she suggested, flipping open the basket.

"Okay. I'll pour while you talk."

"Nothing much to it, really," she hastily assured him. "It just so happens that I, too, eventually ended up in the hands of an older woman—my maiden aunt."

"After things fell apart at home?"

"Yes."

"How old were you?"

The question was gentle, but loaded. She was determined to be truthful, though. "I was sixteen. My mother simply couldn't cope anymore, with me, with reality. She shut herself away. It's my understanding that she's in better shape now. Moved from the state."

Ross gave her a stout plastic cup full of Chablis. "No contact?"

"No." Karen sipped slowly, averting her gaze. "She gave up on me and never looked back."

"Oh, honey, I'm sorry. I—I can't imagine why—how..."

*I was a pregnant rebel, misguided by a most incompetent parent.*

His hand was gently massaging the length of her back. It felt so good. The temptation to let it all out was enormous. But Ross wasn't ready for the news. He was stewing over so many little things concerning Wendy, lamenting over being considered impossible. She hoped the time for her confession would eventually reveal itself. And she hoped she'd be smart enough to recognize it.

"Mom couldn't even handle her own troubles," she finally explained. "I like to think that maybe she just didn't want to cause me any more grief."

"I'm beginning to see why you're so good with Wendy. And why you can understand Margo's effect on her."

Karen sighed softly. "Only too well."

"So this aunt of yours was made of sturdier stuff, was she?"

"From my father's side," Karen clarified. "She commanded respect in much the same way that Grethal does. I guess seeing Grethal in action simply reminded me of her."

Ross caught the past tense in her words. "She die?"

Karen nodded forcefully, gazing down at the rushing stream, glittering in the sunlight. "Her passing sort of spurred my visit here. It seemed like the right time to do some exploring, expand my horizons. Take some chances."

"Your aunt hold you back?"

"Sort of. She was grounded in practicality, you see. Never diverted from her rituals. She did have a thirst for knowledge, though. A remarkable respect for learning." Karen sighed, drawing her knees to her chest. "Guess she'd understand my reasons from that angle anyway."

Ross sensed a lingering hesitancy, a regret, as though the uttering of every word was like a tooth extraction. But there was an unmistakable sincerity behind her revelations. But it was so hard for her to share! Why?

"You know, Karen, I've really been shook up since we made love."

Her smile was apologetic. "I'm sorry, Ross."

"No, don't be," he swiftly cut in. "Our encounter, our separation... The whole thing has left me with one certainty. I am falling in love with you."

She turned, a smile touching her every feature. "And I with you."

He took a long draw of his drink. "I also feel exhilarated and lost."

Karen rapped his arm. "You're supposed to, silly."

"I'm not accustomed to it," he complained. "And I'm not used to a woman so generously giving me the floor all the time, either! You haven't pushed any useless prattle on me even once. I don't know your sign, or your alma mater, or your favorite kind of cheesecake."

"I like mine with cherries on top."

"Yeah, me too," he automatically agreed. "But isn't this the point where you're supposed to be overflowing with intimate details?" he bleakly wondered. "Falling into my arms with babbling abandon?"

"How about quiet abandon?"

With that husky offer, Karen tossed her empty cup into the basket and climbed into his lap. Straddling him, she wound her legs around his lean hips. "How's this for intimate?"

Ross drained his drink in a burning gulp as she rocked into the cradle of his thighs. "Seems like an evasive maneuver," he growled low into her ear.

"I know," she admitted softly. "I'm really struggling right now with a lot of issues and questions and . . . us. I'll work things through eventually."

He raised a hand to her ponytail, shaking loose the terry binding holding it together. "I want to help, honey."

"Then just love what you see, what you know." Karen fastened her mouth to his, plunging her tongue between his teeth for a long, deep taste.

Ross shuddered as liquid fire tore through his mouth and his crotch. She was fluid and alive on him, teasing and tempting with her wet, probing kiss and grinding bottom.

"Could've taken off our clothes," he breathed against her mouth.

"Some nature explorer you are!"

His lids lowered to provocative slits. "Just wait."

Karen shivered as his hands slipped beneath the hem of her red tank top, grazing her loose breasts. His fingers were cold from handling the chilled bottle of wine and brought her nipples to rock-hard peaks. She squeezed the corded muscles of his shoulders through his thin T-shirt as he cupped her bottom, rotating her over and over his solid arousal.

The friction caused by their clothing was a wondrous erotic foreplay. They fondled and caressed each other without removing a thread. Karen rode his lap for the longest time, undulating them both to a frenzied level of need.

It was Ross who reached for the zippers, pulling aside fabric with trembling fingers.

"No wonder you've been stalling," she breathed with a laugh. "Your briefs aren't silver like your Jeep!"

"Made ya look, made ya look," he said chuckling.

The rest happened in a heartbeat. His rigid flesh sprang free and Karen swiftly swallowed him up inside. They came to a wild, urgent climax in the seated position, still fully dressed.

Spent and dazed, they finally tumbled to their backs on the blanket.

"Always a surprise," he said hoarsely, reaching out to stroke the golden reams of hair spilling out over the blanket.

Karen rolled her head to his heaving chest. "Remember that I love you, Ross. Above all else, always remember that."

He groaned into her hair. "How could I ever doubt it, songbird?"

# 11

THE FRANTIC CALL FROM Margo came just as Ross was drifting off to sleep Friday night.

He released an involuntary groan as she began to babble on without so much as a hello.

"Margo, you know I prefer to sleep from two till eight. It is now—" he craned to read the digital numbers glowing on his nightstand "two-thirty."

"There's no time to worry about your damn sleep!" she shrieked. "You are the most selfish man on earth!"

An obvious entrée for some sort of favor.

He sat up with effort, struggling to focus in the dimly lighted room. "Margo, do you realize what day is dawning on us?"

"Doom!"

"No, it's Saturday! May fifteenth. Our baby's birthday."

"Oh."

Ross was happy to hear a breath of remorse in her voice.

"Look, you don't want me there anyway—"

"Undeniably true," he cut in. "All the more reason for me to concentrate exclusively on her today. She deserves a loving atmosphere free of all turmoil. Get it?"

"Do you think I like begging you for help? Like some—some—panhandler?"

He sighed hard, feeling a niggle of remorse himself. "All right, Margo. I'm listening. What's the matter this time?"

"There are going to be arrests in the phony chip operation. Maybe as soon as today!"

"But you are innocent, right?" His voice was groggy, but guarded.

"Yes! But I don't know if they'll believe me, Ross! The police, I mean."

"The Vegas police?"

"Yes!"

"But if you've done nothing—"

"This is a felony, Ross! And they've requested me down at the station twice for questioning. Oh, if they come to pick me up at my apartment—" She bit back a sob. "Do you have any idea how humiliating it will be? It might make the papers. I'll die. Absolutely die!"

Ross picked up a marked slur in her speech. "Where are you?"

"At home."

"Really? This is your party time."

"I'm hiding at home, you fool! I can't think about anything but this trouble."

"What do you want me to do?"

"Fix it!"

"How?" He couldn't keep the anger out of his voice. She was so obviously swimming in self-pity and alcohol.

"Find out if they're coming for me," she sobbed back. "Look here, I'm cooperating about Wendy."

"It's only been a few days, Margo—"

"I know! But I've decided to stay away from her until she wants to see me. Can't you return the favor by checking this out?"

He groaned inwardly. It was a six-hour drive to the desert city. "Yes. Okay. I'll make an appointment with someone in charge down there first thing in the morning."

"Call me right after!"

"Feel free to thank me now."

"This is for you, too," she retorted with a sniff. "We both know you don't want my name linked with this."

Before Ross could respond, the dial tone buzzed in his ear. He set the phone back on the nightstand and sank beneath the covers with a disgruntled noise. His baby didn't deserve this on her birthday and neither did he!

TO HIS RELIEF, Chief Bradley had been more than willing to fit him into his morning schedule. Ross was grateful. He'd left well before dawn and hadn't called ahead to the station until he was halfway to Las Vegas. The chief couldn't have been more cordial on the phone, or now, as Ross was entering his plain but cheery office.

"Nice to finally meet you, Mr. Chandler," he said heartily, moving forward to shake his hand. "Please, have a seat."

"Thank you." Ross smiled at the burly man with the lumbering walk and large sunburned features. His quarters were just as unpretentious, with slate gray furniture and white plastered walls full of framed photographs and certificates. This was a man who was clearly accustomed to plain, straightforward talk.

"You said something on the phone about the counterfeit chip investigation," Bradley prompted, settling back into an ancient steel chair behind his desk.

Ross eased into one of the old wooden slat chairs opposite him. "Yes."

"You have some information for me?" he demanded earnestly. "I'd be obliged, sir."

Ross shook his head slowly, studying his blunt fingernails for a moment. "I am actually here on behalf of my ex-wife, Margo. . . ."

They talked on for thirty minutes, clearing the air. When Ross rose to leave, they were both smiling.

"Don't think twice about taking up my time, Chandler. I understand. You could apologize for not having any information to strengthen my case, though," he added wryly.

Ross chuckled. "It sounds as though you've got what you need, and that you've rounded up the right people. Margo's got a laundry list of problems, but she's not a criminal."

"I know of the lady and the circle she runs with," Bradley assured him with a solemn nod. "We did consider them for a while. Even watched them for a while. But quite frankly, it's turned out that this operation is strictly professional. No amateurs are involved, believe me. Would've cracked it open a whole lot sooner if there had been."

Ross nodded, moving toward the exit. "These things are always tougher with experts."

The intercom on the desk buzzed sharply, and the chief excused himself to answer. Ross wandered over to the wall to examine the framed photos hanging there while Bradley barked out a list of instructions to some-one.

"Sorry, Chandler," he said moments later, joining him at the wall. "Chandler?"

It took Ross some time to connect with his voice. He was in a stupefied world of his own, gazing into the surprising world of Karen Ford. She was in three of the group photos. One seemed to be of a picnic event—a three-footed race with potato sacks. The other two were formal group shots. Of uniformed police officers.

She worked for the county, all right. She was a Las Vegas cop.

"Ah, yes," Ross said as casually as he could manage.

"I hate to rush you along, but I have pressing busi-ness." Bradley shook Ross's hand again and ushered him to the frosted-glass door. "Always feel free to con-sult me. Bye now."

Ross sat in his Porsche in the station parking lot for long minutes, absorbing the enormity of his discovery. Bradley hadn't hurried him out of there because he was busy. He'd done it to get him away from those pictures of Karen! But he'd been too blasted late! Ross had seen and he knew.

Karen was up at his resort spying, attempting to get a line on Margo!

Chief Bradley was most likely on the telephone right now, terminating her assignment.

What she wouldn't do in the line of duty!

She'd played up to him in the most deceitful way, in-filtrating his defenses through his weakest areas: his empty love life and his needy daughter.

Ross gripped the steering wheel with a surging fury. The gall of her betrayal made his stomach churn sour.

He had to swallow hard to keep the bitter taste from rising to his mouth.

Well, she wasn't going to just slip away without a taste of his wrath, not if he could help it. He swiftly started up the Porsche and roared out into the street. At the first red light, he picked up his mobile phone. With a grim profile, he punched in David's number at the resort.

"Yeah. It's me. I've got a rush job for you. I need a more thorough background check on Karen.... I know it's Wendy's birthday! No, damn it, just do it. And I'll help you along with new information. She's a Vegas cop.... Of course I know what I'm saying! Use some roundabout way that won't tip off the people down here.... And don't say one word to anyone. And that means Dinah, too! Oh, yes, and Dave, don't let her leave the grounds.... I don't know if she'll try, but— I don't care! Just handle it!"

Ross pressed his finger over the disconnect button on the phone and his foot down harder on the accelerator. Talk about undercover work! The lengths she'd gone to slip inside his defenses!

No wonder she was so reluctant to reveal personal data.

And Wendy. His poor sweet baby. She'd attached herself to Karen and Karen had let it happen—had encouraged it to happen. Ross's knuckles went white on the wheel as he envisioned the creamy column of Karen's throat in his hands.

"Surprise, surprise, songbird," he muttered, taking a sharp turn onto the freeway entrance ramp. "You're going to be chirping to a whole new tune when I get through with you."

"WE'VE GOT BIG TROUBLE, Karen!"

Karen stared mutely at Dinah, standing in her doorway with a huge box in her arms. She swallowed the remains of her bagel and opened the door all the way. "Come in."

"Sorry to bother you so early," Dinah apologized breathlessly, galloping into the suite. "But being Wendy's birthday, it's no ordinary morning."

Karen leaned into the door to close it, eyeing the other woman in perplexity. Dinah sank onto the small sofa in the sitting area, dropping the box on the cushion beside her. "Get a look at this!" she exclaimed, prying off the cover.

Karen's mouth sagged open as Dinah peeled back some tissue and whisked out a furry white suit with a zipper up the front. "What is that?"

"Bunny pajamas for Wendy."

Karen gawked at the garment for a long, bleak moment. "Why, it's . . ."

"This is Ross's birthday gift to her."

"Oh!" Karen covered her cheeks with her hands. "Oh, no."

"A messenger delivered it to my room first thing this morning. Ross wants me to wrap it up for him. Bring it over to the lounge for the party."

Karen moved in for a closer look. "It has feet."

"It has ears!" Dinah squealed, shaking the hood.

"This is worse than the limo rides," Karen declared soberly, her hands on her hips. "Where did he find it?"

"Had it custom made," Dinah replied. "He said he was having some sort of a surprise whipped up. Oh, Karen, he must be so proud of himself."

"Now where on earth would he ever get an idea like this?"

"He always says she reminds him of a little bunny in the morning."

"A lot of fathers feel that, but to act on it . . ." Karen shook her head in disbelief. "Poor Ross."

"Poor Wendy! She can't open this up in front of her friends this afternoon! She'll die. Absolutely die!"

"Mmm, yes." Karen tapped a finger across her mouth. "Her dilemma is far more urgent than his."

"Don't get me wrong, Karen. I do sympathize with Ross. Wendy's been growing up lately in lots of small, subtle ways. He doesn't mean to hold her back, but he just can't accept that it's happening."

"I think he's working on it a little bit," she said on his behalf. "He's shucked the limo rides in favor of a sedan."

"Thanks to you!" Dinah enthused. "That's why I've come here for help. He listens to you. You're the first woman to have any influence."

"Oh, c'mon," Karen objected with a wave.

"Don't you see? He's really interested in you. And I think it's wonderful. You're his hope for a future, a second chance to extend his family." Dinah rolled her eyes. "He has so much fatherly love to give, he needs to spread it out a bit. On more children!"

Karen felt a hot, self-conscious flush climbing her face. "It's only been a few days," she mumbled.

"You've accomplished more in a few days' time than any other woman's managed to do in a few weeks, a few months—"

"A few years," Karen broke in teasingly.

"Nobody's lasted that long," Dinah countered, poking out her tongue.

"Ross is wonderful, but . . ." Karen wondered if she should confide her own doubts.

"But what?" Dinah persisted.

*He might not want me once he really knows me.*

"I seem to be under his skin half the time," she offered in lame excuse, "like an uncomfortable rash."

"All the better," Dinah assured her. "He's been sort of sleepwalking through relationships since the day I met him. He's generally so urbane, so unaffected by the world around him." She released a joyful laugh. "It's about time that somebody get him hot and bothered enough to spout off like a steam engine!"

Karen sighed hard, pressing her fingers against her mouth. This whole day was so overwhelming. Her child's celebration of life. Ross's interest. She would have to get a grip and hang on. This was Wendy's special day. By all rights, she was nothing more than an interested observer.

"So just what are you going to do to bail out Wendy?" Dinah fretted, busily stuffing the outfit back into the box."

"Would you like me to speak to him?" Karen asked.

"He isn't here!" Dinah lamented. "I called all over this joint. Nobody seems to know exactly where he is or when he's coming back. Of course, David does. But he refuses to spill."

"Count your blessings," Karen advised. "If Ross hadn't been lured off, he probably would've wrapped this gift with his own two hands. And we wouldn't have had the chance to intercept it."

"True, true," Dinah agreed.

"But by that same token, I guess it will be up to us to replace it with something else. At least for the party." Karen cast a fond look at the fluffy garment. "There's nothing really wrong with the jammies. I think it would flatten Ross not to give them to her at all."

"You're suggesting that maybe he could give them to her later on," Dinah deduced.

"Yeah. It wouldn't send a childish message, if he'd already given her an indisputably grown-up gift at the party for her peers to see."

"Good thinking. But where are we going to come up with a replacement in these final hours? I got her a couple of videos she wants, but they aren't going to knock her socks off and sure aren't important enough to put Ross's name to."

"I have just the thing," Karen announced to Dinah's surprise. "Hang on a minute."

Karen disappeared into the bedroom, quickly returning with a small black velvet box. "This is going to be my gift to Wendy. Adding Ross's name to the card will be no problem at all."

Dinah cracked open the box, gasping in awe at the opal pendant set in a sterling silver scalloped oval, hanging from a slender chain. "Gorgeous! Absolutely divine." Dinah gazed up at Karen in wonder. "When did you have time to shop? I mean, you couldn't have known . . ."

Karen shrugged off Dinah's admiring look. "I didn't shop. This happens to be a piece of family jewelry."

"Then you can't—"

"It's more sentimental than pricey," Karen assured her. "But I think Wendy is ready to value something that is not especially expensive, don't you? And it beats the bunny suit," she added on a teasing note.

"Right you are!" Dinah enthused. "It will impress her friends. And I agree that she's ready to take good care of this. To appreciate the affection behind it."

"Well, that's settled then," Karen said brightly. "We'll get some paper and wrap both of these packages."

Dinah rose from the sofa, stretching her long arms above her head. "I still can't believe Ross took off today of all days."

Karen's eyes twinkled over possible explanations. "Maybe he has another surprise up his sleeve."

ROSS RETURNED AROUND three, heading directly for his casino control room.

David greeted him with a sober look. "Let's take this into your office."

Ross ushered him inside, shutting out the other employees and machinery by shoving his paneled door into place.

"Margo called a couple of times," David began, dropping into a chair. "Told me everything with a little coaxing."

"I called her from the car. Explained that she's in the clear."

David nodded. "Good."

Ross edged a hip onto the corner of his desk. "So what have you got for me?"

"Karen's still here. Of her own free will. She and Dinah have had their heads together most of the morning with Grethal, organizing Wendy's party."

The news startled Ross, who was sure he had her moves figured. "You check on her calls?"

"Yes. First of all, nobody called her today to warn her off or anything else. And she didn't call anyone, either."

"But . . ." Ross prodded, noting David's discomfort.

"She's made two calls since arriving here. One was to the law office of some Las Vegas lawyer. The other was to Bradley's direct line."

"That seems to cinch my suspicions," Ross said grimly, closing his fingers into fists.

"What are you going to do?"

Ross forced a mirthless smile. "Nothing, for the time being."

David's bushy brows jumped. "What?"

"I've given this some thought," his employer went on to explain. "As long as she's still here, with every intention of singing at Wendy's party, I'm not going to say a thing."

"Think you can pull off an acting job like that?"

Ross shot him a rueful look. "Have to try. For Wendy. This party means the world to her. Whatever her motives, Karen has given me some new insight into Wendy's needs. I've given Wendy so much, but somehow blindly sidestepped some of these social issues, like peer acceptance. Karen promised us this performance, and I'd rather she deliver with a genuine joy. There'll be plenty of time to sort things out afterward."

"Wendy will eventually have to be told that Karen's been here under false pretenses. I mean, the kid is bound to wonder why her good buddy, Karen, isn't writing."

"One crisis at a time, please," Ross moaned, hanging his head. But he knew there was no chance of separating the tangle of issues involved. Karen had taken them in for selfish reasons of her own. And the fallout was going to be incredible. Despite his anger, Ross was fully aware of the fact that he didn't understand any of it clearly enough.

"You know, Dave, I can't help marveling at the uselessness of this undercover job. Margo wasn't even involved in that counterfeiting mess. And she spends such a small fraction of time here."

David inhaled sharply, putting Ross on the defensive.

"All right, Dave. It has occurred to me that the cops might have thought I was solidly connected to Margo and her pals. We know I'm not, but who knows what sort of line she spouts down there."

"Ross, doesn't it seem rather odd to you that the cops would go to so much trouble to nab insignificant little Margo? Even if she was up to her eyeballs in it?"

Ross's scowl darkened. "Are you suggesting that Karen was exclusively after me all along?"

"Yeah, something like that," David admitted. "I'm sure she would've taken Margo in, too, as a bonus. But I think you were her target all along and that she seduced you to get inside your head."

Ross shook his head in forceful denial. It was just too painful to accept. But secretly it had occurred to him on his ride back this morning. The very idea that Karen had led him on, all the while suspecting him of wrongdoing, was slowly burning a pit the size of the Grand Canyon into his already breaking heart.

THE PARTY HAD BEEN in Dinah's good hands since its inception, so Ross didn't show up at the lounge until the stroke of four. He was struggling with his feelings and hoped to make as little contact with his people as possible. He didn't want to reveal himself. Or risk spoiling one moment of his daughter's milestone day.

No matter what his faults in the parenting department, Wendy's well-being would forever remain his main focus.

Despite all his good intentions, despite his position as owner of the whole shebang, Ross felt he was stepping into foreign, uncharted territory. In counterpoint to the Starlite Lounge's usual romantic evening ambience, the circular room was ablaze with light for this afternoon's pandemonium.

The word "pandemonium" kept tumbling through his brain as he strolled down the ramp leading to the tables. His eyes grew wide as he absorbed the sights and sounds. High-pitched laughter, the shuffle of feet, the banners of flying hair. There were approximately twenty girls in attendance, but it seemed triple that number.

"Dad!"

Wendy emerged from the center of the crowd, a vision in a minty green dress and shiny yellow hair.

He held out his arms, fully expecting her to scoot into them for a huge hug. She slowed down as she advanced, however, strolling up in a reserved way, daintily clutching one arm.

"Happy birthday, baby," he crooned in her ear.

"Thanks, Dad. So how do I look?"

Like a lady. Ross swallowed hard as she took a step back for inspection. All of a sudden, she was all grown up. From her sleek French braid, to her tunic-style dress, to her subtle leather flats.

"I guess the days of patent leather and pigtails are gone," he murmured with a pensive sigh.

Their eyes locked in a twin twinkle full of mutual love and understanding.

"Karen helped me get ready," she confided. "We kept waiting for you to show up, too."

"Business kept me away," he explained. "Had to clean things up so I could be here for the bash."

Wendy released an endearing sigh. "Yeah, I thought so. But I've been waiting all day to talk to you about Karen. Like, what's going to happen to her now? There's no show tonight because of this party, so her job is really over."

"There's not much I can do, Wendy," he said soberly. This was only the beginning of the questions, the demands, the disappointments bound to haunt him. He felt terrible, helpless.

"You have to find a way to keep her here," Wendy declared fervently.

"How?"

"I don't know! You can always fix things." Wendy inhaled, her mind obviously racing. "Give her Tiffany's job for real."

"I can't," he denied on a pleading note. "I have a contract with Tiffany, and Karen really isn't good enough for the permanent position. And as she said herself, this musical thing isn't her career goal. She has some sort of job with the city."

"There's a better way," she said in a mischievous singsong.

"Oh, you are growing up!" he teased with effort. "And your friends are waiting for you," he said, gesturing over her shoulder.

"Oh, Dad, I love you so much!"

But he wasn't going to get a huge arm-looping squeeze out of it. She kissed his cheek, patted his chest and flew back to the cluster of chicks. Ross watched them for a while as they gathered around the gift table, gesturing to the packages, urging Wendy to guess their contents.

The youngsters were different sizes and shapes, but they all held that aura of teenagers-in-training. It was only right that Wendy keep up in all ways, Ross mused, reinforcing the idea in his shell-shocked mind. Best that she be a part of whatever was happening around her.

She was so excited about those little presents. Doubtlessly they were little trinkets, worth relatively nothing, but she picked and weighed each package as though it held gold bullion.

He searched the table for his huge flat box. In one single flash of insight, he realized that his gift was not there and that it was the wrong kind of gift.

"Hi, Daddy darling."

Karen's sultry greeting took him off guard. As did the brush of her lips against his own.

"Karen." His hand was shaking as he pressed it against her back. The fabric of her dress had a crinkled, silky feel under his palm. An inviting feel. A feel he would miss, along with a whole lot of other feelings.

"I saw Wendy race up for inspection," she confided playfully. "Thought I would do the same."

Ross scanned her with a small smile. Her makeup was starkly dramatic as was necessary for stage work. She wasn't in one of her more lavish gowns, however. Rather, she'd chosen a lantern-shaped, knee-length dress striped with bold rainbow colors.

"You like?" she asked, doing a quick pirouette.

He loved. He hated her game, but he couldn't stop caring, wishing she was the image she projected.

Why was she still stringing him along?

Why hadn't Chief Bradley called her to tell her it was all over? That Ross was innocent and just may have seen her in his police photographs?

"Ross? Are you all right?"

Ross blinked from his reverie to find Karen regarding him with concern.

"Yes, of course," he assured her in a low, even tone. "This is all overwhelming. I mean, my baby's reached ten."

*Our baby, darling.*

"Lots of time, agony and effort are behind all the joy," he confided on a husky note, keenly gauging her face for a glimmer of remorse. Her expression was difficult to read. He was certain he was reaching her. But it wasn't shame reflected in those sapphire eyes, but a misty blue shimmer of satisfaction. She seemed to understand, just as she had all along. But how could she?

Karen was overcome by the power behind his words. From his manner, she could swear that he was attempting to handle an incredible loss. "You know, Ross, this is only the beginning for you and Wendy. The more she reaches out, the more she'll have to share with you. I know you'll do right by her always."

An interesting exit line. He gave her a tight smile. "Is Dinah around? I wanted to speak to her about my gift."

"Ross, I should—"

"Sorry, songbird, there's the meal," he interrupted, buffering his words with a pat to her arm. "We'll have plenty of time to talk afterward."

Karen watched him move toward the catering staff entering through a side door. Prowling elegance in his dark, double-breasted suit.

Why did she have the sinking feeling that he was walking away from her, rather than walking to his duties? Perhaps it was just the ultrasensitive state they were both operating in. Each in a separate, private world, coping with the same uncertainties.

Karen so desperately wanted to cross the secret line between them. And the clock was ticking. She was due to leave tomorrow on Sunday. Slotted for duty first thing Monday morning.

She made the impulsive silent vow that she would tell him the truth after the party. The worst he could do would be to turn her away. She knew she had no right to reveal herself to Wendy without his blessing and would honor that ethical imperative. Whether he'd be willing to reveal himself as Wendy's adoptive father seemed to be the biggest question.

Somehow there had to be a way to continue being a part of their life. She didn't want to let the magic among the three of them completely slip away.

Ross was giving her some mixed signals. He still seemed to care a great deal, but had once again retreated into his own sober world. For whatever reasons, she wasn't knocking his socks off in this final hour.

It was a tough adjustment for a woman who courageously went out and conquered the dragons in her path.

Of course, Wendy was the most important point in the triangle. Her happiness and well-being had to come first.

The next three hours passed quickly. The girls were treated to a hamburger dinner with all the trimmings. And Karen sang. Songs from her show, requests from the young audience. The atmosphere was lively and carefree.

At the end of her set, she summoned Wendy to the stage and led the crowd in a rousing round of "Happy Birthday." It was a moment Karen would never forget. The chance to wish her daughter a happy birthday on this sunny May day had been a decade-old dream come true. She knew her eyes were welling with tears and she knew she was squeezing her a little too tightly in front of everyone, but she couldn't help herself.

Her baby was all right. Very all right.

Ross, seated at a table in the background, found his throat closing at the exchange between Wendy and Karen. Wendy had a firm grip on Karen's hand and was urging her down the bank of steps near the table laden with her presents.

What was the woman trying to do to them?

Ross watched the girls pop up from the tables and rush over to watch the ritual unwrapping. He unobstrusively rose from his chair, viewing it all from a detached distance. Wendy had forbidden him from zooming in with a video camera, but he'd had the place rigged with three, and was recording every word, every angle, for posterity. He would watch it all later on.

Karen had a 35mm camera of her own, Ross noted. A camera and a gift of her own. Most likely one that was far more appropriate than his had been, he thought with a wince. He had eaten with Dinah at his out-of-the-way table while Karen took the stage to sing. As he had suspected, Dinah had realized ahead of time how unsuitable the bunny suit would be at this gathering and had kept it out of circulation.

To his ire, she had not replaced it with something more fitting. She reported that Karen would be adding his name to her gift.

The nerve of the move galled him. But Dinah had been so elated about it, so certain he'd be pleased, that he'd kept silent.

"Ross! Join us!"

An automatic smile swiftly crossed his face as Karen hailed him. She was seated at Wendy's left, admiring each gift along with Wendy. He moved in to stand behind them, placing a hand on Wendy's shoulder.

"I'm going to open your present now, Dad!" she excitedly said.

Her hands were trembling as she pulled the wrapping off the small square box, running her fingers over its black velvet surface.

"Go ahead, honey," Karen gently urged.

Wendy popped open the lid to reveal the opal pendant. "Oh, it's so pretty. It's old, too, isn't it?"

"Yes. Do you really like it?"

"Oh, yes," she breathed in awe.

"It's far from priceless," Karen explained for Ross's benefit. "But it is sort of a family heirloom. I really want you to have it, Wendy. Kind of a coming-of-age symbol from your dad and me."

Ross churned with confusion as the surprises just kept on coming. All the signals she was sending were so far from the truths stacked up against her.

In essence, her behavior was right on course with the image he'd built of her: a sincere woman interested in them, an affectionate woman longing to cocoon them in her love.

But the facts stood firm.

It had to be a lie.

His expression remained pleasantly passive as the logical explanation hit him. And he just couldn't wait to hit Karen with it, too. Right between the eyes.

# 12

"ROSS CHANDLER, PLEASE repeat what you just said?"

Karen asked the question in amazement later on that evening in her hotel suite. One look into his dark, dangerous face and she knew. The party was over in more ways than one.

"I think you understand me completely," he grated. "I know the necklace is a consolation prize. Something to soothe your conscience, damn it!"

Karen eyed him impatiently. "Are you mad about the bunny pajamas? Do you think I was trying to upstage you?"

Ross's brown eyes hardened, following her as she moved to the small coat closet in the alcove. She tugged open the mirrored door and reached up to the top shelf for his box. "Here it is, wrapped and ready," she said, moving back to thrust it into his arms. "I know she'll love it. It just wasn't right for the party, that's all."

"This isn't even important!" he lashed back, tossing the box on the sofa.

"Then what is important?"

"I know the truth about you, Karen Bradford. I have it all figured out."

Her eyes widened in bleak surprise at the sound of her real surname. "Oh . . . I see. I was planning to tell you tonight, Ross. Really."

He made a doubtful noise. "I actually found out quite by accident. Happened to be down in your territory this morning and tripped right into it in your Chief Bradley's office."

"But he doesn't know—"

"Doesn't know just how far you've gone," he cut in. "Don't worry, I didn't let on about our personal involvement."

She threw her hands into the air. "It's none of his business! None of it is!"

But he wasn't absorbing the meaning of her words. "Actually, the photographs on the wall gave you away," he confided. "Spotted you in them."

"I see." But she really didn't. Chief Bradley believed she was on a bona fide vacation. She was sure of it. "What led you to him, of all people, Ross?"

"Of all—" He was taken aback by the silly question. "Seemed like the obvious step for an innocent man."

"Innocent man?" she repeated in bewilderment.

"Yes!" he lashed out, dissatisfied that she wasn't quaking under his lethal look. "Once I saw you in the pictures, I realized that Bradley wasn't dealing completely straight with me, so I let David loose on your background. He dug a lot deeper than our usual employee check. And there were your two phone calls from here at the resort to fill in the picture."

Her heart hammered in her chest. Good lord. So he did know.

"How you can possibly justify the games you play with other people's lives...?" His accusation trailed off tightly.

"Do you really think that I consider this a game, Ross?" Her voice was gasping now, as a veil of anguish fell over her features.

He'd finally hit a deeper nerve. But to his surprise, the impact paralyzed rather than vitalized him.

They stood toe-to-toe, locked in a tremulous gaze full of anger, betrayal and fear.

"All I can say is that celebrating with Wendy today has been thrilling," she eventually essayed.

He wasn't expecting the shift in subject, but he was swift on the uptake. "You made today, this whole damn week, just too thrilling, Karen. You made yourself so attractive to Wendy that she wants you in her tomorrows!"

"Well, good! Isn't that good, Ross?"

He regarded her blankly, dumbfounded.

What did he expect? This was exactly what she wanted to hear!

Her mouth pulled a grim line at the obvious answer to her own question. He didn't want her to be thrilled because he didn't want to reveal himself as the adoptive father! She understood the selfishness on an intellectual level, but found it a personal affront. After all the closeness they'd shared.

"How dare you invade our lives, pull our strings?" he ranted on brokenly.

"I certainly never meant any harm," Karen assured him with a helpless flutter of hands. "Look, I came with the intention of staying one week, keeping the truth to myself. I didn't expect to fall for you. I didn't expect you to find me out!"

"How dare you say you've fallen for me?" he challenged harshly. "When every word out of your mouth has been a lie!"

"Not every word," she sputtered hotly. "I will, of course, move on as planned, but I do think I have a right to know just what you are going to tell Wendy about me. What truths you intend to reveal."

He drilled her dewy eyes with driving steel. "Shall I tell her that you came here to spy on us? That you took me in like a prize chump with some undercover hanky-panky?"

Karen didn't know she was going to slap him. She reacted without thought, her hand snaking up to soundly smack his cheek. The noise snapped through the room like the sharp pop of a balloon.

His gaze remained steady. His fingers twitched to massage the burning, but he kept his hands at his sides. "You're quite a marksman, Officer Bradford. You not only hit the heart, but also managed to get inside first to pinpoint its weakest spot."

"I didn't mean to!" she cried back. "You can't know how hard it was to come here, unsure of what was waiting for me!"

"I can understand duty," he assured her. "But once you got close, couldn't you tell that I couldn't possibly be involved in that chip operation?" He raked his hands through his hair with a groan. "How could you take your job so far?"

"You don't know who I am at all!"

"The hell I don't!"

"No, Ross, no," she insisted pleadingly. Her heart hammered as she frantically tried to piece together his train of thought. He knew she was a cop and assumed she was here under cover to spy on him. If she wasn't so flabbergasted, she'd be downright lethal.

Like it or not, this was the time to tell him the truth. She clasped her trembling hands together, steepling her fingers under her chin. "I am Wendy's birth mother."

The announcement was a blunt, stunning blow. His rage swiftly brought him around, though. He'd never been so tempted to strike a woman in return.

"I'm beginning to see your point of view now," she babbled on. "You're under the mistaken impression that I'm here officially to investigate the counterfeiting ring. But that isn't even one of my cases. What's more, Chief Bradley doesn't even know I'm here. As far as he's concerned, I'm on a well-deserved vacation. You see, much of what I have told you is the truth," she explained. "My aunt Irene did just die. Her final struggle drained me physically and emotionally. And then there was her deathbed admission. Actually, it was a hint of an admission," she amended. "She led me to believe that the child I was carrying ten years ago at the age of sixteen had been stillborn. Well, I guess her conscience finally got to her and she hinted that my baby lived.

"Don't you see, Ross? My search led me here to Wendy."

"No!"

Karen's thin, tawny brows jumped in surprise over his instant denial. "Yes! Can't you see the resemblance between us?"

"I don't know if your mistake is genuine, or if this is some sort of shakedown, or if you're simply trying to get out of here in one piece—"

"You just don't want Wendy to know she's adopted," she blurted out fiercely.

Ross grasped her by the forearms, giving her a shake. "Karen, Wendy is mine."

"Legally—"

"Naturally, totally mine! Margo gave birth to her." Ross cringed as tears coursed down her cheeks. She was in obvious pain. But no matter how sincere she might be, this was a tragic mistake on her part. "Now," he began on a quieter note, "you may find it was a different scenario. You may have a baby elsewhere—"

"Were you at the birth?" Karen cut in abruptly.

Ross inhaled sharply. "No. I was in Cannes. Ron and I were setting up the second resort."

Karen gasped in triumph.

"But Margo was very pregnant when I left. Bitched and moaned her way through every minute of it. All for me. Perhaps that bit of insight will more clearly explain why I've tried so hard with her, Karen. Despite all her shortcomings, she created Wendy."

"No, she did not!" Karen sobbed with a stomp of her foot.

"It actually saved our rocky marriage at the time," he went on to admit.

"It's no wonder she needed my baby so urgently, no wonder the transaction was so costly and quiet," Karen mumbled half to herself. "She was fooling everybody, fighting for her life-style."

"What are the chances of you leaving without a fuss?" he asked stiffly, fighting to subdue his temper.

"Excellent odds," she swiftly assured him. She jammed his box into his chest and marched mutely toward the door to see him out. "If you don't mind, I'd like to pack now. I came here to check up on my baby, and I'm satisfied that she's doing just fine."

Ross paused in the doorway, regarding her with a bewildered shake of his head. "Of all things, I never thought, never dreamed you—"

"I know you think I'm wacko," she returned tersely. "But I know what I know. I just hope—" she squeezed her lips to bite back a fresh sob "—I just hope you'll keep my image rather shiny in Wendy's eyes. Even if it's just for her sake."

He nodded curtly. "Yes, I will. For her sake. If you stay the hell away from her for the same reason." Without another word, he was gone.

"What a charming surprise, darling!"

Margo opened the door of her Las Vegas apartment Monday afternoon to find Ross on the threshold.

"Hello, Margo." He breezed past her, reaching out to shove the door closed. "How's tricks?"

"How's your little protégée?"

"You know she's gone." Ross had wandered over to the window and was staring out at the distant desert. His own world seemed as vast and fathomless as the view.

"Karen Bradford. Protégée cop." Margo's satiny purple caftan billowed as she whisked up behind Ross, driving her hands along the collar of his gray oxford shirt. He turned around to brush off her exploring fingers. "Imagine, a slip of a girl like that being a policewoman. Imagine, that girl infiltrating your, ah, corporation...." She drawled out the innuendo, her dark blue eyes falling to his pants. "Something's slipping, lover. Slipping down far too easily these days."

Ross gritted his teeth. He expected just this sort of harassment. Everyone had jumped to the obvious conclusion concerning Karen and her spying—the very same conclusion he himself had jumped to about the counterfeiting. He looked a fool, but protecting Wendy from any possible fallout was his major focus. No one had breathed a word to the girl about Karen's real occupation.

At the same time, however, he'd found he could not dismiss Karen so easily. She had niggled into his heart. Wounding it perhaps, but certainly not killing it, as he'd told her. Now that he'd simmered down, he was judging her more clearly and fairly. He loved her. And when she'd tried to assure him of her sincerity, he'd been too dense to appreciate it. As outrageous as her claim was, she had been genuine in making it. Had been so damn sure of her facts. Her words haunted him day and night.

*It's no wonder she needed my baby so urgently, no wonder the transaction was so costly and quiet.*

She'd made the utterance half to herself, as though verifying the facts for herself.

And as it happened, she seemed less and less like a madwoman with every passing hour. Once his fury had subsided, he couldn't help—with Wendy's unassuming aid—reliving all the wonderful moments they'd shared over the past week. If the impossible was to be considered probable, so much fell into place. Her real grief when speaking of her late aunt. Not fitting in at school because of a sad home life. He could only imagine what it would've been like to be pregnant at sixteen without the support of loving parents. She must've felt so alone, so apart from her peers.

It was something she didn't want for her own daughter.

It explained her rush to help Wendy out. She knew she had only a single week to make a difference.

Unless, of course, she managed to fall in love with the adoptive daddy and turn everybody upside down!

It had taken some selfless soul-searching to come to terms with the possibility that Wendy might not be related to him. He wouldn't love her any less, of course. Sharing a bloodline had just been a natural assumption, something he took for granted. But highly unnecessary.

And if Karen was telling the truth, she was just the sort of altruistic mother Wendy so desperately needed. The kind of wife he yearned for in his dreams.

He only knew he would throw himself on her mercy if she was right. If she was wrong, he would find out just what did happen to her baby.

Either way, he would win her back.

Ross sized up Margo, who was fluttering her long lashes at him and eyeing him like a hungry black cat. She wanted her old open-ended allowance back and she wanted a tumble in bed.

All he wanted was information. There were several ways to get it, but Margo was the quickest. No blood tests, no private eyes, no headlines. If she had a cache of compassion for anyone other than herself, he would've appealed to it.

As it was, a bluff was best. She was so wrapped up in her own desires, he'd run it past her before she could get her bearings.

"So, you came here for tea and sympathy?" she goaded, running a hand through her short cap of hair. "You sounded rather dejected on the phone. I'm sure she was more trouble than she was worth," she airily placated him.

"Trouble to both of us," he casually remarked, folding his arms across his chest.

"How so?"

Ross clucked. "Didn't you recognize her, Margo?"

"As a Vegas cop?" she returned sweetly. "No, I can't say I did. And surely you can't expect me to know them all. She was your little spy. You should've found her out a whole lot sooner."

"I would've identified her more quickly, shuffled her off sooner, if you had been more observant during your visit."

"What?"

"Her real name is Bradford, Margo. Ring any bells?" His ex-wife pursed her lips, lurching with inner revulsion.

"You know I don't care to share Wendy with anyone. How do you think I feel about an adoptive mother catching me by surprise—"

"Ohmigod!" She clamped a manicured hand to her mouth.

"You strongly want your allowance reinstated," he purred in understanding. "But now it looks like I'll have to spread it on the Bradford woman, just to keep her away from my child."

"But she couldn't just— Wouldn't dare—"

Ross's heart jackhammered in his chest as he watched her play of emotion. She was as guilty as hell. Karen had really hit the target.

"You know damn well, Ross Chandler, that you can well afford both of us!" she raved, flailing her arms in the air.

"As it happens I don't intend to pay either one of you anything," he informed her tersely. "You don't deserve it and Karen didn't really ask for it."

"What do you mean?"

"I mean this has been a trick to get at the truth."

She absorbed the news like a physical blow, her features twisting in fury. "Oh, I'll bet big daddy wasn't happy to hear that his precious wasn't his after all. I'll bet he threw his protégée right out the door when she tried to tell him."

"Wendy is mine!" he roared, aiming a thumb at this chest. "In every sense of the word!"

She paced around the room, bobbing her head. "Yeah, well, I made you believe it. Went to a hell of a lot of trouble for you!"

"Why, Margo?" he asked her slender back on a low, perplexed note. "Why did you do that?"

"Because I was losing you, fool!" she exclaimed, whirling around with blazing eyes. "I thought if I gave you the child you so desperately wanted, you'd love me all over again. But our baby boy just didn't make it. Never took a breath."

Pain rocked his body. He'd had son and didn't even know it. Didn't even have a chance to mourn the loss. His features and fists pinched tightly as he absorbed the blow. "When, Margo? How?"

"While you were in France," she lashed back. "I went into premature labor at home. My doctor raced over to the house to assist in the birth. It was no good. I arranged for a burial and I started combing the state for another baby. Baby Bradford just happened to be right on time for me. That old lady, the aunt, she was itching to make the sale. And I heard enough to know they weren't even going to tell the teenage mother the truth. It was all the better for us, of course. I figured she'd never look for her child then."

"But you never took to the baby!" he thundered in grief.

"I realized soon enough that I was being punished for my lies," she returned bitterly. "Wendy quickly stole all of your affections away. You never cared for me again. Not in the same way you once did."

"That wasn't the baby's fault!"

"If our baby had just lived," she calculated reproachfully, "or if I'd have managed to find you a boy, maybe everything would've been different."

"No, no, our relationship was troubled even before then. I was shocked when you turned up pregnant. I thought the only papers I'd be receiving from you would be divorce papers."

"But you got a birth certificate with your name in the father slot," she asserted angrily. "You got what you wanted and you still didn't love me anymore."

The fact that she knew nothing about real love was a point he didn't care to argue. "I think we both know that we should've divorced long ago," he maintained, struggling for calm firmness. "Before the issue of children ever entered the picture. Nevertheless, know now that you've yanked me around for the last time. We're through once and for all. But I want all the details on my son. Get them to my attorneys fast. Your next alimony check depends on it." On the verge of breaking down, he stalked to the door.

"You really should be thanking me, Ross."

He paused, half-turning, a cynical curl to his mouth. "Excuse me?"

"If it wasn't for me, you wouldn't have Wendy and you wouldn't have Karen. I can tell you love her, you know. It's been years, but I remember that look."

"Forgive me if I pass on the platitudes. I believe Karen and Wendy were destined for me. We probably would've connected even sooner if it hadn't been for you. If you recall, I spent a lot of time down in Las Vegas a decade ago. I might have seen a troubled teen and helped her out, waited for her to grow up for me." With that, Ross kept walking, closing the door on a frenzied barrage of insults cursing him to kingdom come.

ROSS PULLED HIS SLEEK Porsche to a purring halt in front of Karen's modest stucco home just before six o'clock on Wednesday.

"Are you sure this is her house?" Wendy wondered, peering out the passenger window.

"Yes, baby, I'm sure." Ross was well-informed about this house of Irene's and a whole lot more. He'd mustered up the courage Monday morning to call Judge Franklin Stewart's office. Ross had figured that Stewart, being one of the only people she'd contacted during her resort stay, most likely played a major role in her life. The hunch had paid off in spades. A bit of candor and well-placed questions to the judge had evolved into a very satisfying, detailed dialogue.

Tough and tender.

Impulsive and shy.

Karen was a bundle of exciting contradictions, an intriguing blend of heredity and environment.

The bottom line had been difficult to broach. Did the judge think Karen would agree to see him? And should he bring Wendy along?

Judge Stewart had given him an emphatic yes on both counts. Karen had returned a lost lamb. Inconsolable beneath her tough shell.

Ross knew how all of that worked through his own darling daughter.

"I wonder if she's really home?" Wendy blurted out in doubt.

"She is." Ross reached over and pinched her chin. "Since when do you doubt my word? Where's your unwavering faith? Unquestioning worship?"

Wendy giggled into his mockingly stern face. "Guess it's the age."

"Thirty-five isn't old! I still have the touch."

She huffed in exasperation. "My age, silly!"

"Ah, yes. Preteen madness."

She rolled her huge blue eyes. "Dad . . ."

None of this had been left to chance, but Ross didn't feel the need to explain that to Wendy. Judge Stewart had a standing invitation to Wednesday dinner and had suggested that Ross stop by then. He said he would help smooth the way. Wanted to see a smile on Karen's face again more than anything in the world.

"Hey, the curtain wiggled," Wendy excitedly erupted, grasping the car door handle. "Let's go!"

THEY WERE HERE. The judge took a fortifying breath as he let the curtain fall back into place over the front window.

"Yoo-hoo!" Karen paused in the living-room doorway dressed in her gray sweats, quilted oven mitts on her hands.

His silver head jerked her way. "What, m'dear?"

Karen blew some stray strands of pale hair off her forehead. "Time to mash the potatoes."

"Oh." Stew stood taller, his normally distinguished air a bit ruffled round the edges. "There's a car outside."

"So? I'm not expecting anyone. Probably for next door."

"No, no," he hastily objected as she turned back into the kitchen. "I've done something. Invited someone over."

"Oh, yeah?" Karen crossed the living room, her mitts raised like a prizefighter, her brows lifted in wariness. Now that she fully understood Stew's capacity for keeping secrets, she found her suspicions automatically aroused. "I hope this isn't one of your strays, somebody who's broken the law and needs an understanding cop."

Stew clasped his hands behind his back and paced nervously. "No, no. I just felt you needed a helping hand, a bridge over troubled waters—"

"Good lord, you're looking out for me again, aren't you?" she lamented in a squeak. "Taking responsible action again, aren't you?"

The chime of the doorbell saved Stew.

"Aren't you going to get it?" she invited with a sweeping gesture.

He lifted his chin regally. "No. Isn't my business."

"Hah!" She marched to the door and whisked it open.

"Hi! Surprise! It's me!" Wendy flew over the threshold into her arms, cuddling up against her.

"Oh. My..." Karen stroked Wendy's back, staring blankly at Ross over her daughter's blond head. "Wendy..."

"Daddy got me out of school," she babbled on, squeezing her tighter. "Are you surprised?"

Karen swallowed hard against her tightening throat. "Yeah."

"Hi, songbird." Ross reached out and tugged the mitts off her hands.

"Come in," Karen abruptly invited in a startled gasp. "Please."

"Hey, you really are super surprised," Wendy noted, breaking free to roam around the room.

She nodded mutely. "Super-duper."

"You shoulda known we'd come," Wendy said matter-of-factly. "It's been four whole days. I miss you. Are you really a cop? Daddy says you are."

"Yes, I am. And this is where I live," Karen explained. "Feel free to have a look around."

"I feel kinda carsick," Wendy admitted, rubbing her stomach over her loose pink T-shirt. "Maybe I better sit down." She sank into the rocking chair near the window. "Dad drives way too fast," she reported with a tsk. "Got himself a ticket."

"Tattletale," Ross grumbled good-naturedly.

Karen stared at him in hungry wonder. He looked as striking as ever in his indigo shirt and black jeans. But he also looked exhausted. His features were drawn into sharper lines and his eyes had an empty gleam.

"This is Judge Stewart," Karen had the presence of mind to say. "For anyone who hasn't met him yet," she couldn't help adding.

"Say, maybe you could fix my daddy's ticket," Wendy proposed. "He was speeding to see Karen, so he didn't mean it."

"Well, I am semiretired," Stew explained with a wink to Ross. "But I guess we could talk about it. Why don't we have a little chat in the kitchen? Get to know each other better?"

"I want a moment alone with Karen, baby," Ross admitted with a nod of encouragement.

"Besides," Stew continued jovially, "a rocking chair is no place for someone with motion sickness. Come keep me company while I mash potatoes." He took the oven mitts from Ross and steered Wendy into the hallway.

"You her grandpa?" Wendy chirped in exiting.

"Sort of a grandpa by choice," he replied. "Can be the best kind . . ."

Karen pressed her hands to her cheeks, gazing down at her grungy sweat suit. "I am so overwhelmed. Shocked."

"I understand," Ross rasped. "But I just couldn't bring myself to call ahead. I knew I couldn't do this situation justice over the phone. Are you in a forgiving mood?"

Karen sighed, collecting her thoughts. "Of course I was angry at first. The idea that you perceived me as some sort of undercover sex kitten set me off like a Roman candle. But I always sizzle out eventually and study the circumstances. I understand what a lunatic you are concerning Wendy. And I know that Margo's pressure must have been awful."

"Yes, but I'm so sorry for the way I mishandled the whole affair. I jumped to the wrong conclusions—"

"And rode them like Paul Revere on his midnight ride!"

He raised a dubious brow. "Not mad anymore, eh?"

"I'm really not," she assured him with a grin. "And I'm grateful to see that Wendy doesn't know what transpired between us."

"Thankfully! Especially since I'm here to mend the damage."

Karen's expression was wry and tinged with doubt. "Mend it how, Ross?"

"First off, I know that you were right about everything."

She lifted her hands, her mouth slanting slightly.

"Of course, that's nothing new to you, is it?"

"No. I was over the biggest shock before I went to the resort."

"And I haven't been on solid ground since!" he confessed, feeling he owed it to her. "I'm reeling on and on with every blow."

"Ironic, isn't it?" she said softly. "I was on my toes for the entire week, frightened that you were going to recognize me, and you didn't even know that I existed!"

He rubbed the back of his stiff neck. "Your revelations flattened me out. But the first fact to rise out of all the debris was that I really love you!" He stepped closer, curling his hands around her arms. "I realized that no matter how this paternity thing stacked up, I couldn't bear to lose you."

"That's a nice sentiment—"

"Hey, it's everything! The bottom line that should heal this hurt between us. I didn't check things out and decide to give you another look. I realized . . ." He momentarily averted his gaze to search for just the right phrase. "I dead-bang knew, that no matter how impossible your story seemed, that you believed it with all your heart. That you couldn't deliberately hurt me or anybody else with a half-baked notion. With that in mind, I opened my mind to the possibility that . . . Wendy just might be your baby."

Compassion washed over Karen as his chest shuddered beneath her hands. "So you confronted Margo with my story?" she prompted softly.

"Well, no." He slanted her a small, sly smile. "I tricked her into an admission. Claimed that as the birth mother, you wanted a share in the Chandler loot."

Karen gasped. "She fell for that?"

"Of course!" he assured her matter-of-factly. "She thinks in terms of greed and assumes others do, as well. Once she admitted that you even existed, she was trapped."

"I'm glad you did it, for Wendy's sake," Karen murmured. "Now there should be no reason for Margo to be barging into her life."

Ross pulled her closer, pressing her soft curves against his length. "Hey, I did it for all of us."

Karen eyed him dolefully. "Oh? You think *we* have a future?"

"I know we do," he crooned into her ear. "It's my feeling that we were meant to be a family all along. That our paths got separated by a fluke of nature and simply took time to realign and meet again."

"Ooooh, that's pretty romantic stuff," Karen teased, skimming her finger along his jaw. "Pretty irresistible stuff."

"So you will marry me? Help me realign our corner of the universe?"

"Hmm, yes," she moaned against his mouth. "Out of a sense of cosmic duty and lots of other senses."

"Missed you...." He kissed her with a humble hunger, exploring her mouth with wet, hot urgency.

Karen eventually pulled back for a steadying breath. "So what about Wendy, Ross?"

He knew exactly what she meant. The motherly concern was shimmering in her deep blue eyes.

"I want to tell her, Karen. Not yet. But someday soon."

"Can you really handle that, Dad?"

"Oh, yes," he emphatically assured her. "The truth threw me for a time, but Wendy is my girl in every sense of the word. And I really believe that had we made her together, she'd be just the same."

"I only want what's best for her. Always have."

"Me, too. I've already spoken to a psychologist friend about it. She knows Wendy through our social relationship, and feels that we should wait until we're well grounded in our marriage before we make an attempt."

"Sounds right," she wholeheartedly agreed.

"You aren't disappointed?"

"No! It's so much more than I ever hoped for. The idea that she will someday know..." She blinked back her tears of joy. "It's just too perfect."

"Lots of other decisions to make in the meantime," he said, linking her arm in his, steering her down the hallway toward the kitchen.

"Such as?"

"Oh, when we're going to get married, for instance."

"This is Las Vegas, marriage capital of the world!"

"So you're free tomorrow?"

"Yes! After work."

"What?" he squawked. "I'll just have to have another talk with Chief Bradley."

"I'm kidding. Finding a fill-in should be no problem."

"How about a permanent fill-in? I'm hoping you'll consider switching careers, joining my security team."

"Ask her if she wants to sing, Dad," a small voice piped up through the open doorway.

"Oh, no," he heartily disagreed. "This songbird isn't sharing her emotions with all the world. From this day forward, she sings only for me."

## PRESS RELEASE

**Houston, Texas:**

Texas media magnate Martin Foster is stepping down as head of the Foster Entertainment Corporation. In announcing his plans yesterday, Foster stated that one of his children—each of whom currently manages a Foster TV station—will take over. Whichever one achieves the greatest increase in station ratings will inherit control of the network. As a result, media watchers expect the next few months to be "unusually exciting."

*Share the excitement! Let Lorna Michaels take you to Texas. Join the Foster family as Ariel and Chad vie for control...and look for love.*

*The Reluctant Hunk* by Lorna Michaels. Harlequin Temptation #523. Available in January 1995 (Ariel's story).

*The Reluctant Bodyguard* by Lorna Michaels. Harlequin Superromance #633. Available in February 1995 (Chad's story).

**Wherever Harlequin books are sold.**

**HARLEQUIN®**

LORNA-M

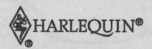

**HARLEQUIN®**

**AMERICAN ◆ ROMANCE®**

This holiday, join four hunky heroes under the mistletoe for

# *Christmas Kisses*

Cuddle under a fluffy quilt, with a cup of hot chocolate and these romances sure to warm you up:

**#561 HE'S A REBEL (also a Studs title)**
Linda Randall Wisdom

**#562 THE BABY AND THE BODYGUARD**
Jule McBride

**#563 THE GIFT-WRAPPED GROOM**
M.J. Rodgers

**#564 A TIMELESS CHRISTMAS**
Pat Chandler

Celebrate the season with all four holiday books sealed with a Christmas kiss—coming to you in December, only from Harlequin American Romance!

HARLEQUIN

*Temptation*

THE
HART GIRLS

Bestselling Temptation author Elise Title is back
with a funny, sexy trilogy—THE HART GIRLS—
written in the vein of her popular miniseries
THE FORTUNE BOYS!

If you missed any titles in this trilogy from
Elise Title, here's your chance to order them:

### *Harlequin Temptation®—Hart Girls*

| | | | |
|---|---|---|---|
| #25509 | DANGEROUS AT HEART | $2.99 U.S. | ☐ |
| | | $3.50 CAN. | ☐ |
| #25513 | HEARTSTRUCK | $2.99 U.S. | ☐ |
| | | $3.50 CAN. | ☐ |
| #25517 | HEART TO HEART | $2.99 U.S. | ☐ |
| | | $3.50 CAN. | ☐ |

(limited quantities available on certain titles)

|  |  |
|---|---|
| **TOTAL AMOUNT** | $ |
| **POSTAGE & HANDLING** | $ |
| ($1.00 for one book, 50¢ for each additional) | |
| **APPLICABLE TAXES*** | $ _____ |
| **TOTAL PAYABLE** | $ _____ |
| (check or money order—please do not send cash) | |

To order, complete this form and send it, along with a check or money order for the
total above, payable to Harlequin Books, to: **In the U.S.:** 3010 Walden Avenue,
P.O. Box 9047, Buffalo, NY 14269-9047; **In Canada:** P.O. Box 613, Fort Erie, Ontario,
L2A 5X3.

Name: _____

Address: _____ City: _____

State/Prov.: _____ Zip/Postal Code: _____

*New York residents remit applicable sales taxes.
Canadian residents remit applicable GST and provincial taxes.

ETST-F

# CHRISTMAS STALKINGS

All wrapped up in spine-tingling packages, here are three books guaranteed to chill your spine...and warm your hearts this holiday season!

**#302 THE KID WHO STOLE CHRISTMAS**
**Linda Stevens**

**#303 I'LL BE HOME FOR CHRISTMAS**
**Dawn Stewardson**

**#304 BEARING GIFTS**
**Aimée Thurlo**

This December, fill your stockings with the "Christmas Stalkings"—for the best in romantic suspense. Only from

HARLEQUIN®

# I N T R I G U E®

HIXM

# SECRET FANTASIES

*Do you have a secret fantasy?*

Chris Nicholson does. A widow, she'd like to find
the perfect daddy for her little girl. She'd also like
to find the perfect lover for herself and explore her
deepest desires. But is all this too much to ask of
Greg? Find out in #522 *LOVE GAME* (January 1995)
by bestselling author Mallory Rush.

Everybody has a secret fantasy. And you'll find
them all in Temptation's exciting new yearlong
miniseries, **Secret Fantasies.** Beginning January
1995, one book each month focuses on the hero
or heroine's innermost romantic fantasies....

...not the same old story

SF-G

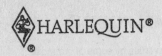 **HARLEQUIN®**

The proprietors of Weddings, Inc. hope you
have enjoyed visiting Eternity, Massachusetts.
And if you missed any of the exciting Weddings,
Inc. titles, here is your opportunity to complete
your collection:

| | | | | |
|---|---|---|---|---|
| Harlequin Superromance | #598 | *Wedding Invitation* by Marisa Carroll | $3.50 U.S. $3.99 CAN. | ☐ |
| Harlequin Romance | #3319 | *Expectations* by Shannon Waverly | $2.99 U.S. $3.50 CAN. | ☐ |
| Harlequin Temptation | #502 | *Wedding Song* by Vicki Lewis Thompson | $2.99 U.S. $3.50 CAN. | ☐ |
| Harlequin American Romance | #549 | *The Wedding Gamble* by Muriel Jensen | $3.50 U.S. $3.99 CAN. | ☐ |
| Harlequin Presents | #1692 | *The Vengeful Groom* by Sara Wood | $2.99 U.S. $3.50 CAN. | ☐ |
| Harlequin Intrigue | #298 | *Edge of Eternity* by Jasmine Cresswell | $2.99 U.S. $3.50 CAN. | ☐ |
| Harlequin Historical | #248 | *Vows* by Margaret Moore | $3.99 U.S. $4.50 CAN. | ☐ |

## HARLEQUIN BOOKS...
## NOT THE SAME OLD STORY

| | |
|---|---|
| **TOTAL AMOUNT** | $ |
| **POSTAGE & HANDLING** ($1.00 for one book, 50¢ for each additional) | $ |
| **APPLICABLE TAXES\*** | $ _____ |
| **TOTAL PAYABLE** (check or money order—please do not send cash) | $ _____ |

To order, complete this form and send it, along with a check or money order for the
total above, payable to Harlequin Books, to: **In the U.S.:** 3010 Walden Avenue,
P.O. Box 9047, Buffalo, NY 14269-9047; **In Canada:** P.O. Box 613, Fort Erie, Ontario,
L2A 5X3.

Name: _____

Address: _____ City: _____

State/Prov.: _____ Zip/Postal Code: _____

\*New York residents remit applicable sales taxes.
  Canadian residents remit applicable GST and provincial taxes.                WED-F

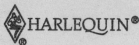

# HARLEQUIN®

Don't miss these Harlequin favorites by some of our most
distinguished authors!
And now you can receive a discount by ordering two or more titles!

| | | | |
|---|---|---|---|
| HT#25483 | BABYCAKES by Glenda Sanders | $2.99 | ☐ |
| HT#25559 | JUST ANOTHER PRETTY FACE by Candace Schuler | $2.99 | ☐ |
| HP#11608 | SUMMER STORMS by Emma Goldrick | $2.99 | ☐ |
| HP#11632 | THE SHINING OF LOVE by Emma Darcy | $2.99 | ☐ |
| HR#03265 | HERO ON THE LOOSE by Rebecca Winters | $2.89 | ☐ |
| HR#03268 | THE BAD PENNY by Susan Fox | $2.99 | ☐ |
| HS#70532 | TOUCH THE DAWN by Karen Young | $3.39 | ☐ |
| HS#70576 | ANGELS IN THE LIGHT by Margot Dalton | $3.50 | ☐ |
| HI#22249 | MUSIC OF THE MIST by Laura Pender | $2.99 | ☐ |
| HI#22267 | CUTTING EDGE by Caroline Burnes | $2.99 | ☐ |
| HAR#16489 | DADDY'S LITTLE DIVIDEND by Elda Minger | $3.50 | ☐ |
| HAR#16525 | CINDERMAN by Anne Stuart | $3.50 | ☐ |
| HH#28801 | PROVIDENCE by Miranda Jarrett | $3.99 | ☐ |
| HH#28775 | A WARRIOR'S QUEST by Margaret Moore | $3.99 | ☐ |

(limited quantities available on certain titles)

| | | |
|---|---|---|
| **TOTAL AMOUNT** | $ | |
| **DEDUCT: 10% DISCOUNT FOR 2+ BOOKS** | $ | |
| **POSTAGE & HANDLING** | $ | |
| ($1.00 for one book, 50¢ for each additional) | | |
| **APPLICABLE TAXES*** | $_____ | |
| <u>**TOTAL PAYABLE**</u> | $_____ | |
| (check or money order—please do not send cash) | | |

To order, complete this form and send it, along with a check or money order for the
total above, payable to Harlequin Books, to: **In the U.S.:** 3010 Walden Avenue,
P.O. Box 9047, Buffalo, NY 14269-9047; **In Canada:** P.O. Box 613, Fort Erie, Ontario,
L2A 5X3.

Name: _____

Address: _____City: _____

State/Prov.: _____ Zip/Postal Code: _____

*New York residents remit applicable sales taxes.
Canadian residents remit applicable GST and provincial taxes.

HBACK-OD